EXECUTIVE DISCLOSURE

EXECUTIVE DISCLOSURE

ISABELLA

SAPPHIRE BOOKS

SALINAS, CALIFORNIA

Executive Disclosure
Copyright © 2012 by Isabella, All rights reserved.

ISBN 978-1-939062-05-5

Editor - Lisa Boeving
Copy editor- Lee Ann Norman

Sapphire Books
Salinas, CA 93912
www.sapphirebooks.com

Printed in the United States of America
First Edition – December 2012

Acknowledgements

To the readers who have been kind to a new author. Michelle, Lori, Reiko, Lisa, Lee, Terry, Sue, and all the others I've met along the way. To say thanks sounds inadequate compared to what you've given me.

To Schileen, my heart soars when you're near!

To my sons, you've given me far more than I could ever possibly give you. Thank you!

Chapter One

The sky turned from shades of blue to the orange and red glow of dusk. Chad readjusted her long body in her seat again. Her daily routine of watching the house diagonal from where she sat for an hour was starting to wear on her. Preliminary work for a job was nothing new. She had done the same thing, on the same street, with the same house at different times throughout the week. Patient, deliberate, and thorough made her good at her job. That's what made her successful. Tonight would be the final phase of the job.

Running through her mental checklist and checking the contents of her bag, she made sure every tool was in place. Dusk had turned to darkness—it was time. Adjusting to the fading sunlight, Chad inspected her backpack and ran through her mental checklist, *latex gloves – check, ski mask – check, flashlight – check, pick set – check*. On and on as she made certain every little detail was rehearsed in her mind. Sliding out of the van, she casually pulled on her knit hat and in one fluid movement she slung the small bag and her warm up jacket on. Slowly, she walked down the street away from the house and picked up into a jog. Chad's unassuming warm-ups and running shoes gave her the appearance of just a woman out for some exercise. She smiled and nodded at a couple walking their dog, then crossed the street and made her way back towards the house she'd been watching earlier. The few streetlights did little to expose her as she made her way to the gate. Bending down, she pretended to tie her shoes and casually looked around the neighborhood.

"Perfect," she muttered.

Quickly darting past the car in the driveway and into the side yard, she pulled down her mask and grabbed her pick-lock set. Adrenaline pulsed through her veins as she got the same sensation every time she did one of these jobs. She easily entered the locked gate and made a mental note of the tall privacy hedge around the yard. So many of the rich and famous wanted privacy, but they rarely thought about what else these hedges really provided. The overgrown foliage shielded the front of the house from view, but would also prevent someone inside from seeing an intruder until it was too late.

Examining the face of the exterior, she ticked off window locations in her head, searching for evidence of cameras or a security system. There was nothing. She had obtained the floor plan easily enough on a quick visit to the building department, and now she was like a kid in a candy store without supervision. Checking around one last time, she noted any windows that might be open or any obstacles that might be in her way. She hated climbing into a two-story window, but if it was an access point then she would risk it. First, she needed to make certain no other options were available. Moving to the other side, she looked for a better opportunity to get in. Nothing.

She made her way to the back of the house, counting steps until she hit the gate. *Thirty-six and a clear path, no obstructions.* She now had a choice: scale the wrought-iron gate, or she smiled, looking through the iron bars—she could just open the unlocked latch.

"Geez, don't these people believe in locking anything?" Chad whispered. She pulled a miniature can of spray lubricant out of the pouch under her jacket. Spraying the hinges, she waited until she was sure they were well lubricated. Slowly, she unfastened the latch, and the gate opened without a sound.

"Perfect."

Chad peered around the corner into the deep, ornate backyard.

"Nice."

She stuffed the can back into her pouch and quietly closed the gate. *I need to get me one of those,* she thought as she slowly walked over to the swimming pool with the built-in waterfall.

No motion lights.

Bending down, she drew her hand through the warm water and brought it up to her nose.

Saline, nice.

Returning her attention to the house, she tugged on a pair of latex gloves. In her line of work, you didn't want to give anything away. All secure in the back, except...a doggie door.

"I don't think so," Chad said.

There was no way she would go in through a doggie door, no matter how big. She gave the face of it a push to be certain. Locked. The dog, like its owner, had left earlier in the day and was not expected back for a week. Standing up, she pulled out a flashlight with a red lens and began to peek into the one window with a half open shade. Following the edge of the window with the light, Chad searched for magnetic tape, wires or anything that would trip an alarm. Darkness concealed her perimeter inspection and allowed her to finish her walk around the ornate structure. She ended up behind the house where she had originally started. This was going to be easier than she thought.

Chad pulled her lock-pick set and began to work through the tumblers. She felt each one vibrate through her fingers as they dropped, successfully unlocking the door. Opening the door a crack, she reached around and grabbed her lubrication to spray the hinges. Although the owner may not be home, she didn't want to set off a noise sensor on the off chance the owner had one. It was doubtful, but in her line of work, she didn't take any chances. Waiting and listening, Chad looked around once more, reviewing the location of obstacles in the backyard in the event she needed a quick escape. Chad still felt her shins ache from the last time she had to rush. A big dog, scattered lawn furniture, and a bruised ego were leftover remnants, courtesy of her last job. Pushing the door open slowly, she made her way onto the service porch and walked into a line of hanging panties and lingerie.

"This is an interesting surprise." Chad fingered a pair of lace panties. "Now why would this woman do her own laundry, with all her money?"

Ducking under the drying line, she walked through a rather ornate gourmet kitchen, an expansive dining room and into what looked to be some sort of library. Books lined the shelves and huge leather furniture dotted the walls. A few pieces of art accented the walls, while a few small sculptures decorated the room, but overall it was rather minimalistic for her tastes. At the other end of the room, she stepped though a doorway to the foyer. To her right was a hallway and staircase, to her left the front door, and directly across from her a double door was partially open. She approached the double doors, peered in, and looked around. This room was vastly different from all the others she had seen so far. Fabric-covered chairs formed a little nook at the center of the room, and flanking the sitting area was a fireplace piled with ashes. The casual warmth of this room gave her a comfortable feeling. When she moved closer to the hearth she noticed a huge pile of partially burnt paper. Chad lifted her mask and pulled one from the charred remains, only to discover not paper, but a picture. Goosebumps rose on her arms as she looked at the photo. From what she could see, it was a picture of a beautiful woman with her arm around someone, and that someone's body and head were burned off.

"Hmm, must have been a bad break-up." Shivering, she tossed the picture back into the ash and circled the room. A photographic memory helped on jobs like this, and she memorized where everything was located in the room. Walking back out of the room, she peered down the hall. Following the stairs with her eyes, she visually made her way around and up the banister bordering the foyer. Slowly, she crept along the outer edges of the steps. The sides would be tight and wouldn't make noise, not that anyone was home to hear it. Old habits die hard and she liked familiar patterns that made her feel comfortable.

Topping the stairs, Chad faced another set of open double doors. Those were her destination tonight. Her purpose – to check out the office inside. To her right ran a short hallway and a longer one to her left. Chad also needed to make a short tour of the rest of the house—nothing more. She had already been here longer than she wanted, so it was time to step things up. Walking forward into the office, she once again pulled out her flashlight and looked around. She marveled at the massive desk that sat front and center in the room. Instead of pointing at the immense picture window overlooking the back gardens, it faced the door directly. *Clearly, the owner didn't want any distractions,* Chad reasoned. The organized stacks on the desk gave her another hint as to the owner's obviously obsessive nature. Looking around, she noted the tasteful and contemporary decor. Peering into what used to be a closet, Chad pulled the door open and saw a ceiling-to-floor safe, some electronic equipment, and what appeared to be a computer server of some type. Everything was organized and labeled.

"Control freak, I'm sure," Chad said, stopping in mid-stride. She heard a sound. At least she thought she heard a sound. She snapped off her flashlight, squatted down, slowed her breathing, and waited. After a few more long seconds, she finally stood and made her way to the door. Inching her head out, she peered around it looking towards the opposite hallway, nothing. Crouching down she peered around again and looked to her right and then again to her left. Nothing. Standing, she went back to work. She needed to finish up and get out of there. Chad didn't spook, but being cautious is what kept her safe.

She walked around a stuffed chair positioned in front of the desk and began to open the top drawer when she heard something again. Now, she was sure someone was in the house.

"Great. Company."

Maybe someone else knew the owner was out of town. *This hadn't been in the plans, but plan for everything,* Chad thought, reaching into her bag and pulling out a roll of duct-tape and a knife. Calmly, she slipped her knife into her front pocket, for quick access in case she needed it, and peeled a strip of duct-tape back, knowing she was going to need that. Crossing the room, she stopped at the doorway when a light flicked on down the hall.

"Amateur. Rank amateur. Now someone will call the police. Shit," Chad whispered.

The sound of drawers sliding open and closed caught her attention. She now had two choices: leave or wait for the idiot to come to her and subdue him. Chad waited and watched as the light went off. She was trained for this kind of thing. As long as the person wasn't taller than her six feet, she knew she had him. Assessing herself, she pulled off her jacket and bag and gently laid them in the corner, out of reach. She didn't want her own equipment used against her. Pulling her mask down, she watched someone walk through the door to her left. The darkness didn't help expose the intruder, but soon he would be close enough to take out. Positioned behind the door, she took measured breaths, flexed her hands, and waited. A moment later the intruder entered the room, stopped, and sniffled.

Sniffles? Great, he's sick. Aw man, now I'm gonna get sick, geez, she thought. Quickly, she stepped behind the man, but paused. The light from the window revealed the silhouette of a woman, not a man. A woman in a short—very short—robe that tied at the waist.

Instinctively, she dropped her tape, stepped behind the shorter woman and whispered, "Don't move."

A few seconds elapsed. "Oh God, please don't hurt me," the woman whispered, "take whatever you want. Please don't hurt me, please."

The pleading sent a chill down Chad's spine and she fought the urge to reassure her.

"Do what I tell you and you won't get hurt." Chad

tried to disguise her voice.

Sudden realization hit Chad that the woman in front of her was Reagan Reynolds, the owner of the home.

Shit, she's supposed to be in Cabo right now. What the fuck?

Chad had seen Reagan leave with her dog earlier in the day. Trying to put the pieces together quickly before Reagan turned around, Chad grabbed a wrist and held Reagan still. Sniffles, it was the only thing Chad could think of now. Clearly, Reagan was sick and had decided to stay home. Chad's mind was firing in different directions at the unsettling development, but she had a job to do and if Reagan blew her cover, it wouldn't look good for her. The police would not be called, period.

"Stop." Chad had her hand on Reagan's shoulders, trying to hold her in place. "Look, don't make me do something we're both going to regret."

Reagan squirmed and fell forward over the back of the overstuffed chair with Chad right on top of her. A firm ass wiggled against Chad's crotch as she tried to steady herself.

"Oh God, please don't rape me. I'll do whatever you want, please." Reagan's desperation was evident in her voice.

"Please, don't flatter yourself, lady."

Trying to disengage herself from the struggling Reagan, Chad gently pulled her arm behind her. The contact with Reagan's ass was starting to have an effect on Chad; she needed to remove herself and fast. She attempted to stand-up, and accidentally pushed on Reagan's back, sliding the silk robe up, exposing her taut nakedness.

"Shit," Chad said, as she finally stood, getting a full view. She grabbed Reagan's other arm and yanked her up off the chair. "Stop struggling, you're only making things worse."

Reagan grew perfectly still. Chad turned her around only to see tears start to fall. *Geez, now she's gonna cry, great.* Chad wiped the tears and looked Reagan in the eyes.

"I'm almost done here, but I can't have you calling the police, so I am going to have to tie you up. Okay?"

She yanked the belt from Reagan's robe and smiled as it fell open, exposing a set of perfectly shaped breasts. Chad tried to divert her attention, but couldn't help herself. She openly admired Reagan's heaving breasts, but before she could do anything else, she felt a sharp pain on the left side of her temple.

"Fuck." Chad grabbed the hand that had struck her and wrenched it behind Reagan's back. The action forced Reagan against Chad, opening the robe further and exposing all of Reagan to Chad's gaze. Dropping the belt, Chad grasped her head, forcing Reagan to look at her.

"I told you to knock it off, now you're pissing me off," she said as menacing as she could sound. "Now, you're screwed."

Turning Reagan around and bending her over the back of the chair, she held Reagan's hand between her legs and wrapped the belt around Reagan's head. Wedging the belt between her lips, she tied it off. Holding Reagan's hands, Chad wrapped the duct tape twice around Reagan's wrists.

"Now, sit down." Pulling the chair around to face the door, she pushed Reagan into it. She winced and rubbed the side of her head.

"Nice right hook you got there."

Reagan gave her a dirty look as if saying screw you and turned away. Chad knew when she was being dismissed and she wasn't playing along. Picking up her flashlight, she aimed it at Reagan's body. Inching the flashlight lower, she made a show of surveying Reagan, reminding her who was in charge. Chad pulled on one side of the robe to close it and accidentally grazed a nipple, which hardened immediately, sending a spike of pleasure through Chad. Reagan's eyebrow shot-up and she tossed a threatening stare in Chad's direction.

"Relax, I already told you I'm not here for that. Besides, you're not my type," Chad said, winking at Reagan and pulling the other side of the robe closed. "You are nice looking, though." Not only was Reagan Reynolds Chad's type, she was sorry they hadn't met under different circumstances. Reagan was petite, beautiful, and even scared, had a spark to her. Gazing at her body again made Chad groan at the lost possibilities.

"The sooner I'm done here, the sooner I'll be out of your hair. So play nice and you'll be fine."

Chad went back to canvassing the room, starting with the desk. As she continued her search, she kept watch on Reagan, who sat staring straight ahead. Finally, Chad realized there was no way she would be able to finish the rest of the house and decided to call it a night.

Walking up behind Reagan, Chad leaned down and caught a whiff of Reagan's perfume, her favorite, Sensuality, by a local fragrance company. Peering over Reagan's shoulder, she could see a partially covered breast and briefly imagined stroking the soft and supple skin. She let her imagination conjure up the image of how it might tighten when caressed. Chad drew a deep breath and briefly chastised herself for letting her mind wander during a job. She needed to get out of the house now before something else went drastically wrong tonight.

"Don't move." She jerked the phone line out of the wall. "Do I need to tie you to the chair?" Reagan shook her head. "Okay, sit there and be a good girl, and I'll let you go in a minute."

Chad grabbed her bag and slung it over her shoulder. Pulling on her jacket, she watched Reagan close her eyes and drop her head. She reached down and gently lifted Reagan's face.

"I'm done, let's go."

Reagan resisted Chad as she pulled her towards the room she had seen Reagan come from.

"Stop struggling. I told you I'm not going to hurt you, come on."

Chad walked into the huge master suite and shined her flashlight around the room. To her left she found the door which led to a massive walk-in closet. She checked the interior to ensure there wasn't a phone, purse, or anything she could use to call the police, and pulled Reagan inside.

"Sit," she commanded and laid Reagan on the floor. "Now listen, don't think about trying to get out. I'll call someone to come let you out so just relax. I'm going to sit outside for a few minutes so if you get any ideas, forget 'em."

Closing the door behind her, Chad pulled a tall dresser in front of the door and sat on the bed, waiting to see if Reagan would try to escape. Yanking her cell phone from her bag, she dialed a number.

"Sir, I need you to come over here and let her out

of the master suite closet." Chad listened to the voice on the other end, waiting until she finally had a chance to respond again. "Yes sir, I thought she was in Cabo, too. Yes, sir."

Chad slammed the phone closed and didn't waste any time getting out of the house. She shook her head and told herself it was the last time she was doing a job like this.

Chapter Two

C had waited in the office while Frank Reynolds finished his phone conversation.

"She's on her way," he said, sitting back in his leather chair.

"How do you think she will take it, sir?" Chad said, distracted by a piece of lint on her gray slacks.

"If I know my daughter, not well," Frank whispered.

Chad took this opportunity to finalize her deal with Mr. Reynolds. Handing over her report, she took great pains to make sure Reagan's father knew exactly what she charged, how she worked, and what she thought it would take to protect his daughter. She was thorough and concise in her planning, leaving little to circumstance. Chad has also made a detailed itinerary, which required strict execution in order to ensure Reagan Reynolds's security. While she could be flexible when the need arose, she also knew she was a step behind whoever was sending the death threats. Chances were the individual or individuals might already know she was on the case, so she couldn't take any chances from this point forward. Checking her watch, as if on cue, Reagan Reynolds stalked into her father's office. Both Chad and her father rose to the impending storm.

"Good morning, Mr. Reynolds," Reagan said. Extending her hand towards her father and waiting.

"Knock it off, Reagan." Turning towards Chad,

he continued, "This is Chadwell Morgan."

"Ms. Reynolds." Chad extended her hand, watching as realization struck Reagan.

Reagan slowly looked her up and down and then struck her across the face. "You!"

"Reagan."

"Daddy."

"Stop it!" yelled Frank. Stepping between the two women, he grabbed Reagan. "She's working for me. Now, sit down and let me explain."

"Geez, she's got a wicked right hook, sir." Chad rubbed the burning mark on her face. "Damn."

Chad couldn't avoid the daggers sent her way, so she focused on Frank Reynolds, who was furiously eyeing his daughter.

Clearing his throat, he started again. "Reagan, as I said before, Ms. Morgan works for us. I sent her over to check the security of your house. Obviously, neither of us knew you weren't on vacation like you were supposed to be, so direct your anger at me, not her."

Chad watched as Reagan pulled her short skirt down when she caught Chad's gaze lower to her exposed thighs. A blushing Reagan seemed to run counter to the spitfire she'd interacted with the evening before. Chad smirked at Reagan's modesty. *I saw a lot more than that last night.*

"I don't understand. Why would you do that?" Reagan's voice gentled as she spoke to him. It was clear to Chad at least, Reagan controlled herself with her father. "What's going on, Dad?"

Running his fingers through his hair, Frank took a deep breath and held it. Obviously, he hadn't told his daughter anything about recent events, and now errors in last night's plan forced him to come clean.

"I hired Ms. Morgan because of some...recent events that have taken place." Frank stood and walked around the desk, leaning on it in front of Reagan. Taking her hands in his, Frank looked down at his daughter with such devotion it made Chad's stomach clench. Clearly, he had tried to protect his daughter by keeping the death threats from her. However, the increased threats now made him fear for both of their safety.

"What recent events?" Reagan looked at Chad and then back to her father. "Dad, what is going on? And why haven't you told me anything?"

"We've been getting the usual hate mail, but lately they've become more ominous, more threatening. So, I hired Chad to check out our security both here at the company and at your house." Frank pulled at his collar; stress etched itself across his already aging face.

"Okay, but why my house?"

Chad somehow wasn't surprised Reagan had caught the slip in Frank's explanation. She had done her homework on the cute brunette. Top of her class at MIT, with a MBA from Harvard didn't make for a stupid woman. It also didn't make for a woman with a lot of time for social skills, the proof still stinging on her face.

"Look, don't bullshit me, Dad. What's going on? Why the hired muscle?" She smirked at Chad. "And I don't use the term lightly."

Chad smirked back at Reagan. Two could play that game if she wanted. Both Chad and Reagan waited for Frank's reply. Chad knew it wasn't her place to tell Frank's daughter anything. He had hired her and he was the one in charge, so she waited.

"The death threats aren't against me. They're against you, honey." Fear suddenly replaced the stress on Frank's face. "I have to protect the company and since I'm getting ready to retire in a few months that means I need to protect you since you'll be the boss. Besides, you're my daughter and that's more important than anything else we could talk about today."

Reagan sat clearly stunned at the news. Disgruntled emails were an everyday fact of life in their industry, but death threats were something that could have some weight to them, they left a trail that could easily be followed. Chad had worked with company executives who hadn't taken the threats seriously and mostly they didn't pan out to anything. But other times they had very nearly cost a company and the CEO their very existence. Boards didn't like the idea of people threatening their livelihood, so they usually took drastic steps to protect their investments. Frank Reynolds was taking the threat seriously for one obvious reason—it was a threat against his daughter.

"I see." Reagan's voice was even softer once realization set in. "Do we have any idea who is behind it?" Studying Chad and her father, it was clear neither could answer her question. "I guess not."

Chad knew the magnitude of the threat couldn't effectively be gauged, so a proactive plan was better than a reactive one. The security at the house was the beginning of what could be a very lengthy, detailed security model. The company had internal securities that required modification, but Chad would work with the head of security—as soon as she checked his background, of course. Then she would implement the procedures for Reagan's personal security.

"Reagan, we're on a time schedule here, remember? You're meeting with each board member personally to get their support on the leadership transition. We don't have much time to get your protection in place." Frank sat back down at his desk, positioning himself as the leader, if at least for image sake. "I need you to be on board with the plans we're implementing. They're for your protection." Frank looked at Chad imploringly.

Clearing her throat, Chad picked up where Frank left off. "Ms. Reynolds. The threats are very pointed. They make it clear, if you take over the company leadership, your life is at stake. I'm sure I don't have to tell you how this could affect the company's position in the market, as well as how the board members might react if they found out threats were being made against your life. It could derail the whole leadership transition. Ultimately, they could veto you taking the helm of the company and place someone else in the position."

Chad had considered every scenario and made her recommendations to Frank. However, he was insistent Reagan would take his place as CEO of Reynolds Holdings, one of the largest financial investment companies in the nation. He had built the company from a meager credit union to the empire it was today, and his dream had been to pass it on to his heirs—well, child. He had hoped to have more children, but when Frank's wife died soon after giving birth to Reagan, it was clear she would be the one to take over. He hoped.

Chad knew women like Reagan Reynolds. They didn't take orders well and were headstrong workaholics. Reagan was also drop-dead gorgeous. Chad couldn't help noticing the shapely, crossed legs that wore a pair of sexy designer pumps. Chad was a sucker for legs and *Reagan's reached all the way up to her ass*, she thought. She chuckled internally. She really didn't know what the expression meant, but had heard her dad say it more than one time when he checked out a woman's ass. His womanizing attitude had influenced how Chad viewed women. Not similar to his—the exact opposite. Her mom had barely survived his philandering before she finally wised-up and divorced him. However, not before he'd shredded their family unit with his drinking and adultery. Chad watched Reagan run a slender hand down her shapely calf. Then she snapped her fingers and pointed upward. Chad had been caught staring.

"Ms. Morgan? Up here." Reagan pointed again up.

"I'm sorry, I was thinking about your issues." Chad said, hoping her lie was believable. Reagan's blue eyes pierced her as she cleared her throat and continued, "I think we need to be on the same page here, sir. I mean, Ms. Reynolds needs around the clock protection, at least until the board vote." Chad made it a point to look at Mr. Reynolds and not at Reagan, whom she knew was casting him a disapproving glance.

His generous salary offer had made her reconsider taking him as a client. Chad had done her homework on Reagan Reynolds and anyone with half a brain would have passed on the job. Reagan's past was historic. With little supervision growing up, Reagan had led a wild life in her teen years. Until her father shipped her off to boarding school. Those years paled in comparison to her university life. According to press clippings, Reagan had spent her share of time on the gossip pages. She had dated almost every rich, eligible bachelor on the east coast. None made it past the first two or three weeks before they were summarily dumped and replaced with a new boy-toy. The only thing missing were the drunken escapades so common with the young, rich, and infamous. Unlike the latest starlets Reagan had kept a modicum of decency. Perhaps knowing she would inherit the largest financial asset in the United States kept her sober in public.

"What are your recommendations, Ms. Morgan?" Reagan laced each syllable with dripping sarcasm.

"Please call me Chad." If looks could kill, Chad would certainly be six feet deep right about now. Continuing, she looked at Frank, "I think we can put a man with Reagan twenty-four-seven, no problem."

"Ms. Morgan—"

"Chad."

"Ms. Morgan, I trust you know your business, but I know mine, and I can't have a man hovering around me twenty-four hours a day. It isn't possible. Besides, someone will notice the meat hanging around my neck." She addressed her father, "Daddy, please."

"I'm sorry, honey. I wouldn't be doing my job as your father or CEO if I didn't put your safety first. End of discussion."

"Ms. Reynolds, I'll be the meat hanging around your neck."

"And why would you do that, Ms. Morgan?"

"Obviously, you don't want a man hovering over you twenty-four-seven. So, I'm more than happy to take personal responsibility for your safety."

"But don't you have work to do here? Didn't I hear you say you have other background checks to do?"

Reagan had boxed herself into a corner with the meat remark, but Chad suspected she needed to prove to the board she could handle the business. More importantly, she needed to prove it to her father.

"Dad, this isn't going—"

"Stop, Reagan. The decision's been made. Now, I suggest you go home and pack. You have a flight to catch. Chad, I'll expect a full report when you land in De Moines, and at every city after that."

Chad knew Reagan was fuming. It rolled off her in waves. She might have won this little battle, but the war wasn't over. Chad was sure by mid-point in the trip, Reagan would be traveling alone and calling the shots, with Chad just a bad memory.

Chapter Three

Reagan fumed at Chad Morgan's patronizing attitude, but more than that, she wanted to wipe the smile right off Chad's face. The way Chad was looking at her made her uncomfortable, considering Chad had practically seen her naked. To make matters worse, she had locked Reagan in her own closet. She and her father would have words after the hired muscle left.

"Dad, you know I have to leave this afternoon for De Moines. I'm sure Ms. Morgan won't be able to book a seat on such late notice." Reagan smiled.

Reagan was scheduled to visit all seven board members before the November board meeting, where her father would name her as his successor. Prior to the meeting, she wanted the opportunity to meet with each member and discuss the company's present path. This was a listening tour, as she called it. Eventually, Reagan would face questions regarding what direction she believed the company should move, but for now her strategy was to keep her eyes and ears open and her lips sealed.

"Please don't worry, Ms. Reynolds. I've already booked a seat right next to you in first class."

"But I haven't booked a seat in first class yet. In fact, I don't know when I'm leaving since it's clear my vacation is off. First class. Dad?"

Reagan couldn't believe the audacity of the

beautiful woman sitting next to her. She wanted to slap the smile right off Chad's face for the third time in one day. What was it about this arrogant woman that rubbed her wrong? Ego, it had to be.

"Ms. Reynolds, I've already cleared it with your father. It allows us to be in a smaller environment, and easier for me to protect you. I assure you, my paramount concern is your safety." Chad looked at Frank for help with his daughter. "Your father informed me of your concerns about your image, and that of the company if you traveled by corporate jet. Trust me, I would have preferred to take my own jet, but I bow to your idea, image is perception."

"Fine." Reagan stuck out her hand towards Chad, offering it as a brief surrender to her situation, but she wouldn't go down without a fight. "I'll meet you at the airport, or do you need to pick me up? I'm assuming I can be trusted to get there on my own"

The soft warmth of Chad's hands cradled her own and forced her to look up when she tried to extract it. Knowing eyes found hers, and Reagan realized right then she would have a hard time persuading her new protector.

"I'll send a car for you. Since I'm now officially *your piece of meat*, I'd like to make sure you're safe." Chad held her grip for another second. "Besides, it's on my way, remember? I know where you live."

Reagan withdrew her hand, furious at the implication in Chad's voice. She despised being second-guessed, she hated being at someone else's mercy, and she definitely deplored Chad Morgan.

"Ms. Morgan, you and I need to have a serious talk about what is and isn't going to happen on this trip." She frowned at her father, then looked back at

Chad. "I'll wait until we're alone and you're defenseless, so to speak." Acknowledging her father again, she stalked out of the office and stopped at Marcy's desk. Her father's assistant had been with the company for years and knew all the family secrets, so to speak.

"Are you okay, Ms. Reynolds?"

"That woman is infuriating," Reagan said to no one in particular as she clenched her fists.

"Are you speaking of Ms. Morgan?"

"Who else? She's an ass."

"Hmm, she has a very attractive ass, if that's what you mean."

Both women looked back through the open office door and watched Chad lean over the desk to point something out to Reagan's father. She didn't just have a nice ass, Reagan noticed, she had a solid body, too. Pushing a wisp of hair behind her ear, Chad turned as if she had heard the two women speaking. Quickly, Reagan turned back around and snatched a piece of chocolate out of the bowl on Marcy's desk. The last thing she wanted was for Chad Morgan to think was she was interested in her.

"If you go for that type."

"Oh, what type would that be? Tall, drop-dead gorgeous and built like a—"

"Marcy. Stop, I get the picture."

"How long has it been, Reagan, since your last date?"

Reagan noticed Marcy was still watching Chad, and then squinted as if she was measuring up the woman.

"Date, date?"

"Date, date."

"It hasn't been that long. What…" Looking

around the room as if she would find divine providence, Reagan tapped her chin with a long, manicured finger. "A couple of months."

"Reagan."

"Okay, a year since my last date."

"Reagan, really I think we need to change your name to that wooden boy whose nose grows when he lies."

Reagan felt the weight of Marcy's disapproving stare on her.

"Okay, a real date? It's been a while. The last time I dated someone who didn't want something from me was a cute little brunette I met while walking my dog at the dog park." Running her fingers through her hair, she slumped down in the chair across from Marcy. "Infuriating, just infuriating."

"Ms. Reynolds, can I see you in here again?" Chad said, her voice dripping with sweetness.

Rolling her eyes and taking a deep breath, Reagan steeled herself for the next round of verbal sparring.

"Cancel the rest of my trip to Cabo, will you Marcy? I doubt I'll be going. If you'll excuse me, it seems the dictator wants to see me."

"Yes, Ms. Reynolds."

The two conspirators were still whispering when Reagan stalked back to the desk. All she wanted to do was go home, take a long soak, and try to forget about how crappy the day was becoming.

"Ms. Morgan?"

"Ms. Reynolds, I've laid out the board members locations and set-up what I think is a more fortuitous route. We can cut down on some air travel by using a car for those board members who are in close proximity to one another, and then finish the trip with nearer locations. All right with you?"

The disingenuous smile from Chad almost made her laugh. She had been around enough 'plastic' people to easily pick out those who were well-meaning and those who were using her for her money. Chad Morgan was using her for her money, but she was definitely humoring her.

"Looks fine to me."

"You're sure? I don't want any surprises down the road. Please review what I've laid out and make sure you memorize the route. I'll make a copy of the itinerary for your father and I'll have a copy. We'll be the only ones to know when and where we'll be going. I'll also make all the travel plans, so staff won't need to be involved in the process." Gathering all the papers and stuffing them in a folder she continued, "The fewer hands in the pot the cleaner the broth."

"Fine. Are we done here?"

"Almost. One more thing, I'll pick you up at six a.m.. I want to get to the airport with plenty of time to go over any last minute changes."

"Daddy."

"Reagan, she's the boss. You need to listen to her when it comes to your safety. It's what I'm paying her for, security."

"Fine." Reagan knew when to fight and when to cut her losses, and right now she was out manned two to one. She kissed her father on his cheek and turned to leave. "Good bye, Ms. Morgan. I'll see you in the morning."

"In the morning then. Mr. Reynolds, I'll call you tomorrow while we're at the airport."

"Have a safe flight and good luck, Chad."

Stopping dead in her tracks, Reagan turned and

gave her father a deadly stare. "Really, father?"

"Good luck, honey. Stay safe," he said, picking up a file and turning towards the window.

It infuriated Reagan to be dismissed by her father in front of the hired help, but she vowed to have the last laugh if it killed her.

Chapter Four

The buzzing alarm barely broke through Chad's sleep-induced coma. She had been up all night packing her bag and preparing her equipment for shipment. She had put a full dossier together for Marcus, her second in command. He usually took care of the loading and packing of the equipment, but since Reagan had made it clear she didn't want a "piece of meat" hanging around her neck, Chad had taken on the task of personal protection and planning for Reagan. She passed on her other cases to Marcus.

Slapping at the alarm clock, Chad only succeeded in tossing it on the floor, with no effect on the buzzing. *Grrr*, she mumbled, tossing the covers back and picking up the clock. Shaking the offending object, she wished it were Reagan Reynolds. The woman needed a good throttling and Chad wasn't sure by the end of the trip she wouldn't be able to accommodate her. Chad flung herself back on the bed, staring at the ceiling. Her body felt like it had missed a meal and rebelled, her stomach flopping around begging to be fed. A slow pain started at the back of her skull, the dull ache probably from sleeping wrong on her crappy pillows. She told herself she would replace them next time she was home, but it never seemed to happen. She looked at the bare walls and wondered when she would finally make this place more like home. If she were honest with herself, she doubted she would ever make the time. It was one of the reasons she worked so much, she was good at avoiding a situation and had avoided this one for the last two years. Spreading her arms wide, she stretched and arched trying to wake up. A glance at her watch told her she was eating into her mandatory workout time. She needed to get moving or take a pass on her daily treadmill torture test.

Walking through the kitchen she pressed the start button on the coffee maker, put two eggs in water, and set them on low to slowly boil. After a quick detour to the bathroom, she came out dressed and ready to work her body almost to exhaustion. Chad stopped at her dresser and picked up the lone picture, smiling at the loving face that smiled back at her. As she did every morning, she stroked the woman's cheek with her finger, caressed her lips and blew a kiss, then replaced the photo on the vacant dresser top. She wiped the same tears pooled in her eyes every morning and went back to her routine. The treadmill run was Chad's time to go through her plans for an upcoming job. Flipping her computer on, she grabbed the remote and touched the huge LCD touch screen above her treadmill. Stepping quickly, she sped up the treadmill, opened the documents she'd created for the trip, and started her workday.

Forty-five minutes later, drenched in sweat, Chad had memorized what every board member looked like, their address, and any other pertinent information she felt might be relevant. Grabbing a towel, she shut everything down, and walked back through the kitchen for her breakfast. She took the eggs off the stove and doused them in a cold-water bath, and poured an oversized cup of coffee. Without thinking, she took a gulp of the steaming liquid, burning her tongue, feeling the scorching liquid move down her throat.

"Fuck that's hot," she said to the empty kitchen.

A single beep from her watch alerted her she had thirty minutes to shower, throw her bags into her car, and get to Reagan's house on time. She was sure this job would be the equivalent to a root canal and cursed herself for being bullied into taking it. After a quick shower, she dried off and ran her fingers through her hair. She would forgo the blow dryer this time for the sake of expedience. Dressing in her standard travel uniform, which consisted of khakis, a button down shirt, and a blazer, she checked her appearance one last time before leaving for what would certainly be a challenging couple of weeks.

꙳꙳꙳꙳

Pulling her SUV in front of Reagan's house, she hesitated briefly before putting it in park. Shading her eyes from the beautiful sunrise, she peeked up the front of the house and tried to see if the lights in the bedroom were on, but couldn't see anything.

"Great, I've gotta go wake sleeping beauty."

Chad cut the distance to the front door in half as she ran, checking her watch at the same time.

"Are you in a hurry?"

Chad practically stumbled over Reagan, who sat on her luggage on the front porch. She peered over the top of a newspaper and flashed a cocky grin.

"I hate to disappoint you, but you aren't going to see me in my bathrobe again."

She wished it were the furthest thing from her mind as she crossed her arms and stood ramrod straight, looking down at the nicest set of legs she had seen since their last visit—yesterday. She had to admit, Reagan was easy on the eyes and had softened the blow a bit when she researched her newest security job. She knew she was in trouble, and could only hope the job wouldn't take as long as she had planned.

"Ready?" Chad extended her hand but all Reagan did was stare at it. Dropping it, she took a deep breath and shook her head.

"When you are."

"Good, let me get these bags for you."

Reagan stood with a smug expression and picked up both bags. "I can handle my own bags, thank you."

"Fine. Let's go, then."

Chad swept her hand wide letting Reagan pass. She smiled at Reagan's arrogant strut, which made her ass bounce. Never one to let a woman take control, she watched the scene play out as Reagan struggled to lift the luggage into the SUV.

"A little help here?"

"Oh, I thought you had those," Chad said, reaching down and tossing the bags into the back. "Next time, let me do the heavy lifting. Besides, I wouldn't want you to get a run in your stockings."

"I'm not wearing stockings."

"Really?" Chad reached for one of Reagan's legs, but had her hand slapped away.

"Don't even think about it."

Chad chuckled and wrung her hand as if the slap hurt. "Don't worry, I was only kidding around. Lighten up or this is going to be a long trip for one of us."

Opening the SUV's door, Chad bowed her head and waited. The slight flash of thigh was her reward for being polite. Reagan caught Chad staring and slapped her on the arm. Without thinking, she slammed the door a little too hard after Reagan sat down. Reagan jumped at the noise and shot her a dirty look. She felt like a dog on the reward system: do something good get a treat, do something bad get an admonishment.

Chad tried to think of something to talk about, but Reagan's body language made it clear she wasn't interested in talking. She was focused on her phone, and the tic, tic, tic of her nails on the screen as she typed something out was starting to irritate Chad. Keeping each other at arm's length would make for an easier trip and keep Chad focused on Reagan's protection, so she didn't push for conversation. After parking the SUV in short-term parking, she began unloading the trunk in silence, when suddenly Reagan came over and helped place the luggage in the carrier. Chad counted four checked bags and two carry-ons. *How did one woman pack so much? Shoot me now, this is unbelievable,* Chad thought, looking at the two bags she had in contrast with the stacked carrier Reagan gripped.

"Let me get the tickets," Chad said, reaching back into the SUV. The last thing she needed was to seem inept when it came to the travel plans on their first day. Chad looked for her bags behind the SUV, but couldn't find them.

"Hey," Reagan pointed to the carrier. "Right here. No sense in you carrying stuff when we have this little handy, dandy luggage cart. Right?"

"Hmm."

Chad wondered about the sudden change in attitude but decided to let it pass. Reagan's entitlement behavior would be a bone of contention soon enough, and Chad knew she would need to pick her battles with this woman.

"Why don't I push this and you can hold the

tickets?" Chad passed off the paperwork to Reagan and glided the squirrelly cart to the baggage check area. Pulling her backpack off the stack, she watched the porter tag every bag, place it on the conveyor and waited until they all disappeared from sight. Turning towards Reagan, she sighed. One problem down, one more to go.

"Why don't we check in and we can hit the bar in the first class lounge? I could use a drink."

"This early? Don't tell me you're a lush."

"Not yet, but I'm sure I'm working in that direction." She grasped Reagan's elbow and guided her towards the security line. "Ladies first."

Chad swept her hand forward and waited until Reagan had her heels off, her bag open, and anything that might set off the metal detector placed in the tray. Pushing Reagan's belongings forward, she stepped behind a woman and small girl who had jumped between them. No problem, she thought. As long as she had eyes on Reagan, Chad was fine being a few feet away while witnessing her hassle the security agent about scratching her new shoes. She pitied the poor man. He never knew what hit him until Reagan sashayed away, swinging her carry-on in victory.

Pulling her loafers, belt, and wallet out, she placed them in the tray and grabbed a second one for her backpack. She pulled out her slim laptop and placed it on top of the bag, waiting for the little girl in front to finish her explanation of how her new shoes lit up every time she walked.

Beyond security, Reagan stood with her hands on her hips, clearly pissed by the wait, but it was unavoidable. Finally, Chad stepped through the metal detector without incident until she felt a hand on her shoulder.

"Stop right there. Whadda ya got, Steve?"

"I need to resend this through, give me a minute."

"What's going on?" Chad looked at the blank face of the security agent staring at the monitor. He flipped the switch on the conveyor belt one way and then the other, pointing at something on the screen and whispering with his fellow agent.

"We need a supervisor over here. I'm sorry ma'am we're going to need to do a pat down."

The agents removed her items from the bins and splayed them across the table. Another security agent reached inside the outer pocket of her bag and pulled two small dime bags of white powder and a large pocketknife. Those weren't her things. She was being set-up and if she had to wonder who would do such a thing, all she had to do was look over her shoulder at Reagan.

"These are not my things. Someone has put those items in there. I'm sure the woman I'm traveling with can vouch for me. Reagan?" Chad looked around but couldn't find the woman anywhere. "Fuck."

"Right, these aren't yours. You wouldn't take a little party in a bag on vacation 'cause it would be illegal. Right?" The man swung the bags in front of her face and then deposited them into a bigger evidence bag. "And look at this knife, it's huge and sharp." The security agent ran his thumb along the blade and before she could warn against it, he sliced his thumb wide open.

"Fuck, I am in the company of idiots."

"Shit. I need a Band-Aid, Steve. This damn thing nearly cut my thumb off."

"Those things aren't mine. I'm telling you someone set me up."

"Sure. Would she be the phantom woman you're traveling with? Besides, you were with a woman and a child. We didn't see you come in with a woman. Nice try buddy. Wanna try again?"

Someone grabbed her arm and the bins with her stuff. They pushed her towards a room labeled "Private".

"We need a swab kit, and a drug kit, and call a female for a strip search."

"Are you kidding me? I want to make a phone call. I assure you I can clear this up in ten minutes."

"Right, you don't think you're the only one to play that game are you?"

"Look, you don't understand, I have to make this flight."

"It looks like you're gonna have to make the next one, assuming everything turns out okay."

Chad scanned the airport lounge looking for Reagan, and found her. She was sitting casually, sipping coffee, thumbing through a magazine, and looking right at Chad. Narrowing her gaze, she zeroed in on Reagan, locking eyes with the cocky woman. Reagan winked at Chad and blew her a kiss before returning to her magazine.

"Bitch."

≈≋≋≋≋

An hour later, the door to the private room opened and a pissed off Chad stepped through, followed by three red-faced agents, a supervisor, and her lawyer.

"I'm going to sue your ass off. Trust me, you haven't heard the last of this, assholes. You're probably all going to be cleaning out the latrines in the airplanes by the time I'm done with you."

Chad slung her bag over her shoulder, and shook her lawyer's hand.

"Thanks for getting down here so quick, Jake. Sorry to pull you out of a meeting with the director."

"He wasn't happy, but he is the one who asked you to take this job. So, he owes you. We need this company to stay solvent and stable. They're the money behind a lot of defense contractors and right now we need all the help we can get overseas."

"Yeah, I know, but have you met Ms. Reynolds? She's a pain in the ass and I'm sure she's the one who put baby powder and a knife in my bag."

"Buddy, you better get a handle on that little gal or she's gonna lose the support of the board and we don't want tree hugger Mason taking over. Do what you have to do to protect her."

"I gotta call the old man now and raise my prices. I told him if she caused trouble it would raise the price."

"Poor bastard doesn't know what a deal he's getting for your babysitting services."

"Don't call me again with another babysitting job. I'm strictly black ops, I'm wasting my talents with jobs like this."

His slap on the back knocked the wind out of her and nearly caused her to go flying. "I know, I know."

"Let's go. I'll buy you a drink till your flight leaves."

"I'm not traveling commercial. We tried it her way, now we do things my way."

Flipping her phone open, she hit speed dial and waited. "Hey Marcus, I need you to gas up the Lear and get all the equipment we thought we didn't need for this job loaded. Yep, there's a little problem, but I'm going to take care of her when we met in De Moines. Have a car waiting at the airport, too. Make sure it has all my equipment and a set of restraints, too. Yes, I'm serious. Okay see you in an hour."

"You gonna make it in time?"

"Yeah she has a two hour layover in Los Angeles and then on to De Moines."

"That should give you plenty of time to cool off."

She shot her lawyer a look. He put up his hands and backed away. "Or maybe not."

He tapped his watch and continued, "Look, Chad I have to go, the director is meeting with the Chinese consulate and he wants me there. Have fun and let me know if you need anything."

"Thanks, Jake. Pray you don't hear from me, cause if you do, it might be to defend a murderer."

Chad couldn't believe she'd been played by a pretty face and a nice set of legs. It wouldn't happen again, not if she had anything to do about it. Marcus would take care of getting her equipment to De Moines, but she needed to come up with a new plan of action, since the kitty had no problem working her way out of the bag Chad had so neatly made for her.

Opening her cell phone again, she called the one person who might be able to handle Reagan Reynolds— the operative word was *might*—her father.

"Good afternoon. Mr. Reynolds. No, I'm afraid we aren't in De Moines yet. It seems Reagan placed some suspicious items in my carry-on and they pulled me from the line. I've spent the last hour trying to explain I didn't put baby power in dime bags, and the rather large hunting knife they found wasn't mine. Didn't even have my fingerprints on it, but it did have Reagan's. Remember the clause in the contract stating if Reagan created any problems during her protection detail the cost would rise for every offense? It just went up two thousand dollars a day."

Chad held the phone from her ear expecting to hear the words of a hostile man, but instead he apologized and begged her to stay on the case.

"Yes, I understand, but you know how your daughter is. In fact, she could have cleared this misunderstanding up, but all she did was wink at me and blow me a kiss. So, you're lucky I'm not raising it five thousand dollars a day. If she does one more thing, you can expect a phone call. Yes sir, I understand. You have a nice day, too."

Chad took a deep breath, hoping to clear her head before she began the task of arranging alternative transportation for the rest of the trip. She mentally chastised herself for dropping her guard. She had completely underestimated Reagan, but she wouldn't make that mistake again. Now, it would be her rules, her ride, and her way or she was off the case and Reagan be damned. If she couldn't understand the reality of the situation, then she hoped her father had connections to get a good protection team in place before something happened. First she would give Reagan a reality check as to the dangers that might lay waiting for her.

"Christopher, this is Chad. I need a flight plan filed and the second set of gear and com equipment loaded and ready to go in an hour. No, I'm not in De Moines already. I'll explain everything when I get to the hanger. Hey, can you send Manny's number to my phone? I'm going to make Reagan Reynolds sorry she pulled this stunt and send a message. Great, see you in sixty." Chad slammed the phone shut and cursed one last time. "This is the last time I listen to a woman."

Chapter Five

Reagan sat back and mentally high-fived herself for successfully dumping Chad Morgan. The baby powder wouldn't get Chad in trouble, but it would get her stopped when they found the two bags. The knife had been an afterthought. In fact, the only reason she had done it was to make sure the TSA would keep Chad from getting on the flight. Reagan figured she would be able to bluff her way around the powder, since any idiot who opened the bag and took a sniff would know it was baby powder. Shoot, she figured Chad would say she put it in her bag for her shoes, blaming foot fungus. Reagan had to be sure Chad would want released from the case, so the knife was the icing on the cake. Turning off her phone in the first class lounge would keep her father at bay until she reached the hotel. Then she would listen to him chastise her erratic behavior and tell her what a fool she was and he had reconsidered hiring a babysitter. It might be wishful thinking on her part, but there was one thing she was sure of: she wouldn't be seeing Chad Morgan again, if the look she flashed Reagan was any indicator.

Chad might have been able to convince her father her life was in danger, but Reagan didn't by it. Why would anyone want to hurt her? It didn't make sense. She was nobody in the big scheme of things in the business world. Almost nobody. Settling into her plush, first-class seat, Reagan turned her phone on, passed the two waiting messages, and flicked through her email. She had called the De Moines office and arranged for someone to pick her up at the airport, so she was set when she landed. Everything else could wait until she reached De Moines. She turned the phone off.

Pulling a magazine from her briefcase, she thumbed through it while waiting for take-off. A small head popping up in front of her caught her attention. The little boy yelled "Hi!" every time he peeked over the seat.

"Hello yourself, little man," she said. The biggest brown eyes she had ever seen peeked at her through the crack between the seats.

Pudgy little fingers pushed through the space and wiggled at her. Reagan touched the little hand and heard a squeal come from the other side. It withdrew and then pushed back through the crack. Clearly, the little boy was playing a game of 'touch me'. Enthralled with the game, Reagan couldn't resist the raucous giggling that started every time she touched the wiggly little digits. Suddenly, Reagan heard the young boy's mother admonish him for bothering the 'nice lady'.

She unbuckled her seatbelt and stood. "You know what, it's my fault," she said quietly. "We were having fun. I'm sorry I didn't mean to get him wound-up."

"I'm sorry, he can get pretty excited and this is our first flight together," explained the young mother.

"No, no please don't apologize. He's adorable. What's his name?"

"Can you tell the nice lady your name?" she said to her son.

The little boy buried his head in his mom's chest and held up three fingers. As he turned his head, she caught a glimpse of his impish smile before he shoved a finger in his nose.

"It's okay if he doesn't want to tell me, I understand. I was shy growing up, too."

"Oh, he's not shy. Trust me. His name is Juan Carlos. We're going to see Daddy in Spain."

"Nice. What a mouthful for such a little guy," Reagan said, patting the young boys head.

"We call him, JC. Isn't that right, honey?"

"It's nice to meet you, JC. My name is Reagan."

"Do you have any children?"

"Oh, no. I'm married to my job. No time, but someday, maybe."

"Don't wait too long. This guy takes all my energy and I couldn't imagine doing it any later in my life," the woman said, before apologizing. "I'm sorry, I shouldn't have said that. I didn't mean you're old or anything. I meant there isn't a right time for kids, I guess."

"No worries. I knew what you meant. If it happens, it happens."

Extending her hand, the young mother introduced herself. "Sheila."

"Nice to meet you, Sheila." The seatbelt light caught her attention. "Guess I'd better sit down. Nice to meet you both."

"Likewise."

Little fingers passed once more through the crack and wiggled at Reagan. The light giggles made her smile as JC's mom pulled him back and strapped him in his seat. Reagan wondered if she would ever have kids. Her life wasn't moving in the motherhood direction and she wasn't taking steps to push it that way. If she wanted to have kids, she needed to find a partner first. She wasn't about to start a family on her own without the requisite other side of the parental unit. Besides, her clock wasn't ticking, it was barely thumping along, and the urge to merge wasn't even part of her vernacular, let alone her mindset. Her father had finally stopped inquiring into her personal life and had resigned himself to the fact she probably wouldn't marry before he retired. The reality was her job was her mistress, and adding a partner would only make her feel like she was cheating on her mistress or worse, cheating on her partner. Oh, how life could be cruel.

❧❧❧❧

The bumpy turbulence only added to Chad's already darkening mood. A rushed flight plan, a quick check of the baggage, and a missed lunch did little to help her disposition, but the thought of scaring the shit out of Reagan put the briefest smile on her face. She hated being bested at her own game of evade and protect and Reagan had shown Chad that trust now had to be earned. Somehow she doubted it would happen before the end of this job. If Reagan thought she was on a leash before, her chain lost a few more links, and Chad hoped she was prepared for the babysitting.

"You're in a foul mood, buddy," Thomas said, glancing away from the instrument panel.

"Yeah, you wouldn't be jumping for joy if you had endured a strip search in front of a seventy-year-old woman."

"I'm sure it was the highlight of her day. Seeing your bare ass all spread out and—"

"Hey, now. You don't need to be so descriptive. I was there, remember?"

"So, grandma seeing you in your birthday suit

got you in a bad mood?"

"Not exactly. Reagan Reynolds has that honor. She dropped a few dime bags in my carry on and then to top it all off, she stashed a hunting knife in the outer pocket," Chad explained.

"Sounds like a piece of work."

"Yeah, that piece of work cost her father another two thousand a day. She's jumped to the top of my shit list. I hope she's good at poker, 'cause I'm ready to call her bluff.

"I'm sure whatever plan you had has changed. Is that why I'm coming along?"

"Yep, she didn't want a piece of meat hanging around her neck. Now she has a piece of meat and more," Chad said, looking at Thomas's bulk. "I can't think of a more intimidating piece of meat, can you?"

They both laughed at the implications of Reagan's bad decision. She had preordained her own fate with her stunt at the airport and now had to pay for her bad decision.

"Lear one-zero-papa. You are cleared for approach, over." The radio squawked breaking the levity.

"One-zero-papa, roger."

After a smooth landing and taxiing to a private hanger, Chad stood and stretched as best she could in the tight confines of the cockpit.

"Geez, we're going to be doing this for the next few weeks, shuttling a little spoiled brat to all her appointments." Chad shook her head, wondering how she had allowed herself to be roped into such a crap detail. "I still need to get over to the other side of the airport and watch her arrival. I've got a little surprise for our Ms. Reynolds."

"Chad. Play nice with the girls." Thomas chuckled.

"Oh trust me, this is no girl. She's a full-on bitch."

"Remember your fee went up two thousand dollars, so it should cushion the blow," he said. "Just a little."

"A little. Okay," Chad spied her waiting car. "I'm out of here. I'll see you at the hotel."

"You got it."

Tossing a duffle and a backpack into the car, she waved at Thomas and ducked into the blacked-out back seat. Now she needed to make sure her plan was set in motion and went off without a hitch. Chad flicked her phone open made a quick call, gave the driver instructions, and waited across from the arrival terminal.

Chapter Six

The flight was long enough that Reagan caught a few minutes to rest her eyes. The gentle prodding of the flight attendant woke her instead of the rambunctious little boy in the next row. In fact, Reagan was surprised he had been so well behaved the entire time. Peering over the seat, she smiled down at the little cherub face sleeping.

"The altitude always gets him," his mother offered.

"Makes two of us." Reagan reached over and gave the mother a friendly pat. "You've done a wonderful job. He's a cute little guy."

"Thanks. It was nice to meet you."

"It was nice to meet you and JC. Travel safe."

"You, too."

Grabbing her carry-on, she strode down the gangway to the terminal and checked her watch. The flight was late, as Reagan expected, and she was glad she had accounted for the possibility. Her instructions for the driver were explicit. She was to be picked up exactly at 12:15, which would give her time to get her baggage and be at the curb waiting. The baggage claim sign was on the other side of the airport. It seemed quite a long way off. Her shoes felt like they weighed a ton as she strutted down the aisle. Now, she wished she had worn something a little more appropriate for travel, but being a slave to fashion, she had opted for something sexy instead. She mentally laughed at her own stupidity. Dressing sexy for whom? Chad? Impossible.

She positioned herself at the baggage carousel and waited for her hot pink suitcases to pop up out of the chute. As the luggage came up and made its way around the turnstile, the crowd moved in closer, and someone tapped her ass. Turning around, she shot the man a glare as he smiled and shrugged his shoulders.

"Sorry."

"Hmm."

Reagan spotted her bag when it popped off the conveyor and traveled away from her. She leaned closer to the rotating luggage and felt a slight nudge. A guy's voice spoke. "Here, let me get that for you." He reached for what he thought was her bag.

Shaking her head, she reached down and grabbed her bag. "Sorry, that's not mine, but thanks anyway."

"Oh, sorry. I should have guessed."

"Really?"

"I mean, well, you're such a beautiful woman. Pink suits you."

"Really?" Clearly, the man was trying to hit on her, but she wasn't easily baited.

"Guess, I'm not doing this right, huh?"

"I guess it depends on what you're trying to do."

"I saw you get on the plane and I wanted to talk to you then, but you were sleeping and well…"

"I wasn't sleeping, just resting," she said defensively.

"No worries. I just didn't want to intrude on your privacy."

"Thanks, I don't get much time to myself, so I took advantage of the opportunity." She didn't know why she was talking to this guy, but he was doing his best to engage her. "Look, I'm sorry, I'm here on business and I don't mix business with pleasure. It sounds like you're looking for something I can't give you."

"Really?" He clenched his jaw before he continued. "You flatter yourself, lady. I was just trying to be kind, that's all."

"Okay, and why have you been watching me the whole time, inventing a reason to talk to me. Right?"

"You can't blame a guy for trying, can you?"

Reagan suddenly became suspicious of his motives. Was he following her for a reason? Maybe he was connected with the death threats, or maybe he was simply flirting with her. Either way, he wasn't going to get anywhere now that he'd shown his hand.

"Well, enjoy your stay in De Moines." Pulling the handle on her luggage, she turned to leave, but felt his hand stop her.

"Wait, how about we get a drink in the lounge?"

"I don't think so. Now if you'll remove your hand," she said firmly, pointing to where he still clutched her upper arm.

She looked up into his face and hoped he could see how pissed she was getting, but then he did something she didn't expect. He put his business card in her blouse.

"Are you fucking crazy? Who do you think you are? If you don't get the fuck away from me I'm calling the police," Reagan shouted at the shocked man. "Get your hands off me!" She jerked away and started towards an approaching security guard.

"Is something wrong ma'am?"

"That man over there put his hands on me." Reagan turned to point, but the man was gone. "He was standing right over there."

"I saw him ma'am, but he's gone. Would you like me to call the police so you can file a report?"

"No," she said with a sigh. "I would just like to get to my hotel."

"Why don't I escort you to your car and make sure you get off without a hitch?"

"Thank you, I would appreciate it," Reagan said, pulling her luggage behind her.

"Let me get that." The security officer took the handle and Reagan's carry on, unburdening her further.

"Thank you so much."

"My pleasure ma'am."

Walking towards the departure doors, Reagan casually chatted with the young security officer. Soon enough his constant chatter made her mentally check out. A woman standing at the doors held a sign with her last name on it.

"Aw, that's me," Reagan said, pointing to the woman.

"Okay. I hope your trip gets better. Welcome to De Moines," he said, passing off the baggage to the woman holding the sign.

"Ms. Reynolds?"

"Yes, are you from the service I called earlier?" The woman raised her eyebrows at the obvious, which made Reagan chuckle. "Of course you are. Lead the way."

The long black limousine was overkill for the short drive to the hotel, but Reagan had been in such a hurry when she booked it, she didn't care what car they sent, as long as she could get to the hotel and get checked in on time. She wanted to get settled and go over her notes about Alex Hamilton, the first board member she would see. Then she would eat and get some much-needed sleep.

"Ma'am?" the chauffeur held the door wide.

"Oh, sorry, I was just thinking about all the things I have to get done."

"No problem. We'll be at the hotel in about fifteen minutes. I hear they have a nice lounge at the top for VIP guests."

"Good to know. Thank you."

"My pleasure, believe me it's my pleasure," she said, smiling before shutting the door behind Reagan.

A low voice startled Reagan. "Hello."

"Hello?" Reagan said pensively

The speed of the car pressed her firmly against the back seat as Reagan tried to focus on the person sitting in the darkness. Her chest tightened in fear and she grabbed for the door handle.

"I wouldn't do that if I were you. The car is going pretty fast."

"Who are you and what do you want?" Suddenly a woman leaned forward pointing a gun at her. "Is it loaded?"

"Aw, it's stupid question day. Okay, I'll play along. Yes, it's loaded."

Looking around the limousine, Reagan tried to assess the situation. Something had gone drastically wrong. If karma was a bitch, she was paying for what she had done to Chad earlier at the airport. Why she would remember Chad at this point was ironic, since Chad had preached to her about travel safety on the way to the airport. She had blindly followed the woman with the sign, gotten into a car without thinking, and was now possibly being kidnapped or worse, killed.

"Please, my father will pay you. Whatever you

want. Just don't kill me, please."

"Okay, take your clothes off."

"What?"

"You heard me. Take your clothes off."

"No."

"I don't think you understand how this works. I have the gun. I get to make the rules. My gun, my rules. Get it?" The woman leaned in closer and ran the gun up Reagan's leg. "Nice."

Closing her eyes, Reagan tried to block out the feel of the cold gun grazing her leg. She couldn't move even if she wanted to, fear had her paralyzed. Her heart pounded in her chest and her hands shook as she raised them in resignation. Finally finding her voice, she squeaked out, "I'm not taking my clothes off."

"I don't think you—"

"I understand just fine. I'm not taking my clothes off, so you'll have to shoot me." The quaking in her voice betrayed Reagan's bravado. "Do what you have to do."

The seat next to Reagan sagged when the woman slid closer. Her hot breath against Reagan's neck was revolting as she whispered in her ear. "Trust me, you don't want to see me pissed off. It isn't a pretty picture." The woman's hand slid up past Reagan's knee before stopping just under the hem of her dress. "Am I making myself clear here?"

Reagan nodded briefly and closed her eyes, suddenly wishing Chad was there. If she hadn't set Chad up, she wouldn't be in this situation. She would only be dealing with an arrogant woman instead of one who wanted to kill her. If she could just reason with this woman, she was sure she could turn the situation around. Taking a deep breath, Reagan turned towards the woman and placed her hands on her chest. She gently grabbed the lapels of the woman's jacket and ran them between her finger and thumb as she slid the back of her hands up down the woman's chest.

"Look, I'm sure we can come to some kind of agreement. Can't we?" Reagan crooned softly.

A smile ticked up the corner of the woman's mouth revealing a dimple. Reagan returned the smile and locked eyes with the woman. If she could play men, she was sure she could play this out in her favor. A mix of fear and success bolstered her to continue. Watching as the woman slid her tongue out and lick her bottom lip, Reagan mimicked the same behavior. Focusing on her opponent's lips, she bit her bottom lip and kept her hands moving up and down the hard chest beneath.

"You're good, but you're not that good." The woman trapped Reagan's hands and pushed her back against the seat. She pressed her firm lips against Reagan's, practically bruising them. The kiss lasted longer than Reagan wanted, but just long enough to show her who was in control. "Now, stop your shit and get you're dress off, since you're so hot to see what happens next."

"But, I'm not," Reagan blurted out. "I mean, I'm not hot. I mean. I don't want to see what happens next. Oh please don't."

The car stopped quickly, lurching forward and sending both women to the floor. Pulling herself up, Reagan tried reaching for the gun and found herself wrestling with the woman as the door opened.

"Are you done?" Chad said, reaching in and grabbing Reagan off the floor.

Chapter Seven

W hat the fuck?" Reagan grunted "Get up."

Pulling Reagan free, she deposited her on the pavement and shouldered halfway through the door of the limousine. "What the hell were you thinking, Rita?" Chad whispered. "I said shake her up, not rape the poor woman."

"I did shake her up. Trust me, she isn't going to leave your sight now. Besides, you didn't tell me how hot she was, she's a scorcher."

"Knock it off, Rita. I can't use you on the job now. She's gonna freak every time she sees you. Get back to the office and send out Eric."

"What? What the fu—"

"Knock it off," Chad said, crouching over Rita. "I told you to scare her, not practically fuck her. Did you think I wouldn't see everything? I had the car wired and I saw it all. Next time you pull your gun you better be using it to protect, not fuck."

Rita turned her face away from her boss. She had taken it too far and now she would be lucky to keep her job. Keeping a cool head wasn't her strong point and had gotten her booted from the FBI, but her tech skills had earned her a job with Chad's security team. Now Chad wondered if she was more trouble than she was worth.

"Sorry," she whispered.

Chad shook her head and pulled the woman to a sitting position. She sat back and stared at Rita, then groaned. "What am I going to do with you?"

"Fire me?"

"Too easy. Get your ass back to the office and wait for my orders. Since Eric is coming out here you're going to have to run his part of the operation."

"Okay."

"We'll talk when the job's over. You had better have a really good reason for what you did, so think long and hard about it and have a good answer when I get back."

"Thanks."

"Don't thank me yet, I haven't said you're not fired."

"Got it," Rita said, dropping her head. "Guess I better apologize to Ms. Reynolds."

"I don't think it's a good idea. She's going to be pretty pissed off when I explain what happened."

"Right."

"I'll email you instructions for the next leg of the trip, so be waiting."

Chad exited the limo and tossed her head in the direction of the trunk. "Can you open the trunk so we can get her luggage?"

"Sure boss," the driver said.

The glare Reagan sent Chad made her flinch slightly. She had some explaining to do, but so did Reagan. In fact, Chad was going to make her squirm for as long as possible. Her reputation had been questioned back at the airport, and she had to call in a big favor to clear it. So, whatever Reagan had to endure paled in comparison. Chad took little care in the way she tossed Reagan's luggage into her own car, slamming the lid with as much fervor as she could muster.

"Thanks Sophia, I'll see you soon. Get Rita back to the airport and make sure she gets on a plane."

"No problem, Chad," she said offering her hand. "Consider it done."

"Sorry you have to babysit."

"Oh, it's not babysitting if you like it."

"Something you need to tell me?"

"Hmm, not yet, but I'll let you know."

Sophia opened the door and waited as Chad pulled Reagan up to the car.

"Don't even think of giving me any trouble after what you pulled back at the airport," Chad whispered. She looked away from Reagan. "Get in."

The dazed look on Reagan's face confirmed Chad's plan had been successful. She had designed the whole incident to show Reagan she wasn't as in control she thought. However, Rita had come on too strong and Chad hoped she hadn't sent Reagan crying to her father, but what was done, was done.

The door closed behind her as she sat across from Reagan and stared at the distraught woman. Reagan was a tissue short of a good cry, so Chad chose her next words carefully.

"Something you want to tell me?" Chad said, pulling small plastic bags out of her blazer pocket and tossing it in Reagan's lap. "Perhaps you can start by explaining this."

Reagan looked down at the little plastic bag filled with baby powder, running her finger along the zipped top before tossing it back to Chad. A long sigh delayed her response as she gazed out the window.

"I told you I didn't need a babysitter."

"Really? You've been in danger from the moment

you got off the plane. Reach into your blouse and pull out the business card."

Reagan's shocked look slipped and she instantly became angry. Reaching into her blouse, she pulled out the forgotten card and started to hand it to Chad.

Chad put her hands up and shook her head. "No, you read what it says."

Turning the card over in her hand, Chad watched her eyes move over the text and the shocked expression return. Reagan closed her eyes and dropped her head back against the tall seat of the limo.

"What does it say?" quizzed Chad.

"Bang, you're dead," Reagan whispered.

Chad reached over and took the card which now lay limp in Reagan's hand. Putting it in the inside pocket of her blazer, she watched the scenery as it passed the limo. Reagan had to start taking things seriously. She wasn't just putting herself in danger; she was risking the safety of Chad's team as well. With each passing minute of silence between the two women the tension in the limo rose. Whether she was embarrassed or pissed didn't matter to Chad. Reagan needed to broach the subject with her, so she would wait a few minutes more.

"How far?" Reagan asked.

"How far what?"

"How far were you willing to go to teach me a lesson?"

Chad watched Reagan's face hidden in partial darkness and studied her profile. She was beautiful, not in a classic way, but the kind of beauty that made men want her. Soft features, a rounded face, and full-lips that pouted when she was mad made her look younger than her actual age of thirty-five. Her hair cascaded easily around her face and neck. Instead of looking messy, it had that bedroom look that made Chad want to run her fingers through the brown soft locks after making love. A touch of make-up completed the soft look.

"I'm sorry it went as far as it did. Rita's on her way back to the office and will do her job from there," Chad explained.

"I see."

"I've scheduled a massage and a facial for you when you arrive at the hotel. I figure you could use one."

"Hmm."

"Do you know how many times you could have been killed or kidnapped from the time you got off the plane until the moment I came on scene?" Chad's hoped her angry tone conveyed her disappointment.

"I don't know two times, I guess." Reagan sounded defeated.

"Nope, four times. The woman with the little boy was a plant. Cute kid, huh?"

"No way."

"Way," Chad confirmed. "He's her nephew and she could have taken you out when you went to the bathroom after your third glass of wine."

"How did you know I had three glasses of wine?" Reagan rolled her eyes and let her head fall back on to the seat again.

"The woman had a small camera in her shirt. I had a nice view of you when you peaked over the seat to talk to Juan Carlos. The second time was when my guy came over and touched your ass. You thought he was flirting, but he was sizing you up. Getting close enough to put this little reminder in your blouse." Chad rubbed her face before continuing. "Do you think every guy wants to get into your pants? Really?"

"You planned this whole thing, didn't you? You knew I was going to dump you at the airport in San Francisco."

"I had a feeling you were going to try and give me the slip. So, I planned for it. I do this for a living," Chad's tone became more menacing as she continued. "People more important than you pay me a lot of money to protect them, their families, and their most important valuable – their lives. I don't have to be just good at my job, I have to be great."

Reagan looked ashamed as she rubbed her hands on her dress, pushing it down closer to her knees. She had been made, so to speak, and now Chad knew she had her right where she wanted her.

"So, want to hear about three and four?"

"Let me guess, the young kid dressed as a security guard?"

"Yep, you were starting to get a little loud and he needed to de-escalate the situation, before a real security guard came over. Never trust someone just because he wears a uniform. You didn't even look at his ID card clipped to his collar. If you had even looked at his badge, you would have noticed it said Honorary Dog Catcher."

"Oh shit. I feel like such a fool."

"You should. You could have been killed five times."

"Wait, I thought you said four?"

"We have two more times to talk about. The fourth time was the driver holding a paper sign with your name on it. The security guard took you right to her. Did you ask to see ID? Did you ask the company you arranged transport from what the driver looked like?"

"No," Reagan slunk further down into the soft leather.

"No," Chad repeated. "You just went with her. She could have shot you on sight, but instead she delivered you right to the last threat. Number five. Rita."

"I had my cell phone in my hand. I could have called 911."

"Give me your cell phone," Chad asked extending her hand. "Give it to me."

Chad slid the face of the phone forward and looked at the number pad. "What number is 911?"

"What do you mean? You hit 911 and it dials emergency."

"So you don't even have it programmed in your speed dial. You think you have time to dial 911 when someone is dragging you into a bathroom to rape you, or down a vacant hallway to kill you?"

More silence answered Chad's question. There was no right answer to her question and she had Reagan over a barrel. Protecting someone who wanted her help made the process easier, protecting someone who sabotaged their own protection detail made for more work and a riskier job. Chad would have to be firmer with Reagan if this was going to work.

"Look, as I said before, I've made arrangements at the hotel for you to have a massage and a facial in your room. Maybe it will help and then we'll go over the rest of your itinerary."

"Fine."

The ride to the hotel was an exercise in restraint for Chad. All she wanted to do was reach over and throttle the woman who she was slowly learning to hate. She could be better utilizing their time together by briefing Reagan, but why waste the time? Reagan didn't have options now, she had to follow the game plan or hire someone else.

Chapter Eight

They lapsed into silence giving Reagan time to think about the events of the past hour. She knew she had plenty to be ashamed of, but she was also pissed. If she were honest, she had to admit for the first time in her life she had feared for her safety. Not all the bravado in the world could have allowed her to bluff her way out of such a horrible situation. Her heart still pounded, and the adrenaline pushing through her veins made her feel like she was on fire. Worst of all was admitting to herself the woman sitting across from her was right. Chad had set everything in motion, knowing she would try to outsmart her, but the only person outsmarted was Reagan. Her pride was wounded, and she should consider herself lucky Chad was only rubbing her nose in it right now. If Chad was looking for an excuse, Reagan didn't have one. Shame was her companion right now, and she didn't like it. She hadn't really thought past trying to lose Chad at the airport, so there wasn't anything beyond that in her mind.

A stinging on the back of her hands caught her attention. Turning them over, she noticed scrapes on her knuckles and a cut ran down the back of her left hand to her wrist.

"Let me see your hands," Chad said, checking her knuckles.

"I'm fine."

"I know your fine. I just want to see your hands."

Chad moved next to her and grabbed her left hand before she could pull it away. Pulling her backpack over, Chad produced a small first aid kit and began doctoring her knuckles.

"Did you get these scratches when you were wrestling on the floor with Rita?'

"Probably."

Reagan flinched when Chad rubbed her thumb across her palm. The warm contact caught her off guard.

"Sorry," Chad whispered, focused on her hand.

Chad lifted her arm and ran her hand along her forearm. The touch was suddenly unsettling and Reagan pulled it back.

"What're you doing?"

"Checking for more scratches, bruises, or anything which might need medical attention."

"So, you're a medical doctor, too?" Reagan asked.

"I've had my share of medical training, but no, I'm not a medical doctor. I can give mouth-to-mouth though. Would you like to see?

"I think I'll pass, thank you. Besides, I don't need to see a doctor for a few scratches."

Reagan waited as Chad applied a wet wipe to the scrapes and examined the scratch more closely. Breaking out a tube of ointment, she applied a few dabs down the scratch and covered it.

"That should do it."

"Thank you, Dr. Morgan. Now I know my hand won't fall off. What would I ever do without your expert care?" Reagan joked.

"If you hadn't dumped me at the airport then you wouldn't be in this position, so I'm glad you can find some humor in it."

"I try."

"Since your mother isn't here would you like me to kiss your boo-boo?"

Reagan looked at Chad, but didn't laugh. Surely, she knew Reagan had lost her mother at birth. She had never had any kind of mother figure growing up, and didn't know what it was like to have that influence in her life. How could someone miss something she never had in the first place?

"I'll be fine, thank you."

"I'm sorry, I didn't mean to be so callus."

"No problem, really."

Reagan dismissed Chad's comment, reaching for her phone and dialing her father.

"Hi, Dad."

She shifted away from Chad and moved the phone to her other side to keep Chad from listening.

"Yes, I got your message, but I was in the air and my phone was off, so I couldn't return your phone call. Then I was kidnapped, and I'm finally able to call you."

"Not really kidnapped," Reagan said, looking over at Chad, who was now sitting across from her.

"Oh, don't worry she's right here." Reagan paused. "Yes, well she must have taken a direct flight to get here. I'll explain everything when I get to the hotel, Daddy."

"Yes, I'm fine. Really. Okay, I'll call you as soon as I get checked in. I love you, too."

Snapping the phone closed, Reagan relayed her father's message to Chad. "He wants you to call him immediately."

Chapter Nine

Reagan's smug expression made Chad smile. If Reagan thought her father was going to rip *her* a new ass, she had another thing coming. If she knew Frank Reynolds, he was checking to make sure she wasn't bailing on his daughter. He had given his consent when Chad explained her plan before putting it in place. She would never have risked his wrath doing otherwise. She would let Reagan have her perceived victory, but it would be short lived. Chad was sure when Reagan finally talked to her father he would lay down the law to her.

God, why did the woman have to be so attractive on the outside and such a bitch on the inside? Is this what working too much did to women, shrivel up their insides and make them old before their time? She hoped she never found out the answer. It would crush her to think this was how her wife, Dawn, had seen her.

The roller coast ride she had been on with Dawn wasn't just filled with ups and downs, it was curving and death defying at times. Their relationship had begun when they worked together at "the firm", and was purely professional at first. Chad was impressed with Dawn's in-depth knowledge of cyber terrorism and the inner-workings of satellite surveillance. She had hacked into a Russian spy satellite and sent the information back to the firm before the country even suspected the security breach. Once the hacking was discovered, Dawn had written the self-destruct code, rendering the satellite little more than flying space junk without a trace back to the firm. Then one day Dawn hadn't reported for work. Chad was informed her mission had been completed, effectively severing their working relationship.

A few years later, Chad had also left the firm to start her own executive protection company. Dawn had suddenly reappeared. For Chad it was a no brainer, she hired Dawn on the spot. They picked up where they had left off. The daily banter, the closeness they shared, and finally, the love, was all back. The years between didn't seem to matter to the other. First, everything gelled well. The field work was challenging, the company grew, but one day Dawn told Chad she wanted out of the field. She said it had taken its toll. Instead she would focus her attention on the day-to-day operations of the office. Cyber security, client contacts—the kind of work Chad hated to do.

Everything flourished, including their relationship. Then suddenly Dawn couldn't get out of bed. She didn't go into work. She hid in her room and slept for days. Chad was shocked. Dawn wasn't Dawn and she refused to go to the doctor to find out what was going on. She blamed their overactive lifestyle and the need for some downtime. For a while Chad bought it, but it became clear early on that Dawn was hiding something. Chad felt helpless with Dawn and finally threw down an ultimatum: get help or she was leaving. They couldn't survive the wild mood swings, the depression, and the pendulum swing to the other side when Dawn worked days on end. When they'd finally gotten the diagnosis of bi-polar disorder, Chad had been relieved. Now, Dawn could receive treatment with the right combination of medications and therapy. Before things started to work themselves out, a wrong cocktail of medications drove Dawn into a deep depression. She committed suicide, leaving Chad behind to pick-up the pieces and deal with Dawn's family and her own emotions.

Chad had been away on a job when she got the call from Dawn's mother. Dawn came from a tight Irish Catholic family and spoke to her mother every day. When her mother hadn't heard from Dawn in two days, she went over to their townhouse and let herself in with her key. Chad remembered how Dawn's mother explained the eerie silence of the house. She heard none of the usual noises when Dawn was home, T.V. blaring, or the radio playing. Dawn's mom knew something was wrong. Dawn hated the silence when Chad was gone on a job. Even the customary lights Dawn kept on for company were off.

Instead of calling the police to check things out, as Chad had always advised, she decided to investigate matters for herself. It would be the last image Dawn's mother said she would see every night for the rest of her life. Dawn's lifeless body hung in the huge walk-in-closet. There had been no signs of a struggle, to perhaps indicate Dawn regretted her decision; no telltale sign of claw marks around the neck, as if she tried to save herself. An empty bottle of Lorazapam laid on the nightstand. The prescription had been filled earlier in the day and every pill was gone. Chad wished Dawn's mom hadn't been the one to find her. A parent should never out live a child, she'd told Chad at the funeral.

Chad blamed herself for Dawn's death. She worked too much, didn't make enough time for Dawn, and had her own version of playtime that often included solitary trips alone to decompress from the stress of her job. Her heart was buried with Dawn the day they laid her to rest. Nothing anyone could say or do would help Chad. She had practically wrapped the noose around Dawn's neck and shoved her. Their last phone call had been painful and brief.

"*Hey Baby, I miss you.*"

"*I miss you too, Dawn. What's up?*" *Chad said, distracted by a conversation next to her.*

"*I miss you. I need you and I want you to come home, now.*"

"*Honey, you know I can't do that. The job's almost over and I'll be home then.*"

"*It might be too late then, baby.*"

"*What do you mean, it might be too late?*"

"*Nothing, I'm just having a tough time with the depression. That's all, I guess.*"

"*Didn't the doctor give you a new cocktail to try?*"

"*Yeah, but I either sleep too much and I'm a zombie, or it wires me up and I sit around thinking all day and all night. She's tweaking it right now, I'm sure it's just going to take time for my body to adjust.*"

"*You want me to call the doctor and talk to her? I mean, I have power of attorney. I can talk to her.*"

"*No, no, I'm sure it will be fine. Besides, she gave me something to take the edge off. I'll just see you when you get home.*"

"*I love you,*" *Chad reminded her.*

"*Yeah, I love you, too. Goodnight.*"

"*Nite.*"

The soft sound of Dawn's voice that night still echoed in her ears. Chad had long forgotten what her laugh sounded like, or the way she giggled when she was excited. No, the only sound she remembered was the long sigh before Dawn hung-up the phone. Guilt was just one piece of baggage she packed every day in her life now. She never left home without it. How could Dawn have done this to herself—left Chad all alone in a world they were building together? Her only guess was Chad hadn't meant that much to her. Ending her pain was more important than what they had together. More than Chad meant to her.

The car's lack of movement jarred Chad back to reality. Reagan was studying her. The expressionless gaze gave no hint to what lay beneath the cool veneer of Reagan Reynolds. Looking out the window, Chad realized they had arrived at their hotel. She opened the door and Sophia stood ready to help her out. Waving her off, she nodded her head in Reagan's direction and gave a quick order.

"Help, Ms. Reynolds out and then make sure her bags are delivered to her suite."

"Yes, ma'am."

"What about your bags?" Reagan inquired nonchalantly.

"My bags and equipment were already delivered and set-up an hour ago," Chad informed her. "Shall we?" Chad swept her hand wide and followed Reagan to the entrance.

Reagan walked towards the front desk, but was guided to the elevators instead.

"I've already checked you in and had your room swept."

"That was fast."

"Yes, well you'll find I'm efficient. I don't like to waste time or energy. So if you'll follow me, I'll be more than happy to show you to your room, Ms. Reynolds."

Chad nodded at the front desk clerk and inserted a key in the elevator panel to open the door.

"A private elevator?"

"Ms. Reynolds. My job is to keep you safe and the only way to do it is to minimize the risk. You have the entire top floor. I've also arranged to have those board members closest to De Moines flown in. They have rooms on the top floor and it will give me a chance to keep you well protected."

"Hmm." Reagan stood rigid in the elevator. "I guess I don't get a say in any of this now do I?"

"Not after what you did at the airport, no," Chad confirmed. "Your massage will be here in about an hour. That should give you time to shower if you'd like, and then I have dinner scheduled two hours afterwards. It should give you plenty of time to relax before we discuss the rest of your itinerary."

As the doors to the elevator opened, Chad stepped out first and surveyed the hallway, motioning Reagan to exit. At the end of the hall, Chad slipped a keycard into the lock and pushed the door wide for Reagan to enter. She checked around the living room and then looked through the bedroom and bathroom.

"It looks good. I'm right next door if you need anything," Chad said, pointing to the adjoining door. Opening both doors, she smiled. "I'm going to leave this open, just in case, of course."

"Of course." Reagan's temper looked as if it was ready to peak. She turned and left Chad standing in the doorway.

Chad slid her blazer off and tossed it in the chair next to the desk, already loaded with computer and surveillance equipment. Shrugging her shoulders, she tried to work out a pinched muscle between her shoulder blades, knowing it wouldn't release until she took off her shoulder holster. The weight of the pistol and magazines pulled on her when she was fatigued and right now she had been up twenty-two hours and counting. She unsnapped the holster and heard a noise behind her. Chad drew her Glock and spun toward the sound. She leveled the pistol. Reagan screamed and threw up her hands.

"It's me, it's just me."

"You shouldn't sneak up on someone. You could get shot," she chided Reagan.

"Is that thing loaded?"

"Of course it is. How can I use it if it isn't loaded?"

"I mean, do you have bullets in it?"

"It's ready for action, if that's what you mean. Yes."

The silence between the two women was uncomfortable. Chad holstered her gun and looked questioningly at Reagan. She watched Reagan's eyes scan her room, taking in her surveillance equipment laid out on the second bed, and then finally stopping on Dawn's picture. Without a word, Reagan fingered the picture frame and then picked it up, studying Dawn's face.

"Do you always go into someone's personal space and touch things that don't belong to you?" Chad snatched the photo away and replaced it on the dresser.

"You went through my room and I didn't say anything."

"I'm paid to protect you and sweeping your room is part of my job. Your coming into my room isn't part of the job description as my employer.

"Yes, well I came in to find out when the masseuse is due to arrive."

Chad checked her watch and calmly stated, "He should be here in about five minutes." A soft knock on the door made both women turn. "Speak of the devil." Chad opened the door and addressed the man in white holding a massage table. "Good Afternoon. You must be Mike. Do you have identification?"

As Chad and Mike exchanged pleasantries, Chad watched Reagan take one last look at Dawn's picture before she went into her own room.

"You can set up in there. I'll leave this door open in case you need something."

"It won't be necessary. I have everything I need right here," the masseuse said, patting his bag.

"No, it will be necessary. Besides, I insist."

"I understand. I'll just set-up and get started."

"Okay, I'll just leave you two alone. I'll be right next door if you need me," Chad said to Reagan and pointed to the open door.

"I'm sure I'm in capable hands, Ms. Morgan. Right, Mike?"

"Of course, Ms. Reagan."

Chad walked to the adjoining door, closing off the conversation behind her, but not before she heard the masseuse say, "If you'll disrobe and slip under the towel, we can get started."

Chad's mind went in ten different directions when she heard it, but her body only went in one. A flame sparked inside her, shooting a trickle of warmth through her. The best thing she could do now was divert her mind and hope her body followed quickly. She dug her gun cleaning kit from her bag and began the process of breaking down her semi-auto. Disassembling her gun in less than fifteen seconds, she methodically laid out each part in order and inspected the pistol.

A man clearing his voice broke her concentration. The masseuse who was supposed to be taking care of Reagan stood in the doorway.

"Is there a problem?" Chad said, noticing the pained look on Mike's face.

Stepping quietly, he moved closer to Chad and cupped his mouth to whisper in her ear. "Actually, there is, my wife just texted me and she's going into labor." He showed Chad his phone.

"Okay, so...?"

"I have to leave right now. I'm so sorry. I really am, but I have to leave. I called my replacement and she can't get here for almost an hour."

"Oh shit, Ms. Reynolds is really looking forward to this massage. I don't think you understand the kind of day she's had." Chad felt bad, but she was practically pleading with the soon-to-be father.

"Ma'am, I am so sorry. I really am, but I have to leave. Ms. Reynolds just laid down on the massage table and she's ready. I just don't have the heart to tell her I have to leave. She...well she seems pretty keyed up."

"Dude, you have got to be kidding me. If you only knew." Chad peeked around the corner of the door, but the only thing she noticed was the tiny towel barely covering Reagan's butt. It seemed so small Chad swore she could see cleavage on top.

"I'm ready when you are, Mike," Reagan said, her face buried in the hollowed out pillow at the top of the table.

"Have you ever given a massage before?"

"Oh, no. No, I'm not a masseuse." Chad threw her hands up in surrender.

Chad had boundaries with clients: don't talk to a naked client, don't touch a naked client, and don't be in the same room with a naked client. Period. She never, ever crossed those boundaries and she wasn't going to start bashing down those walls tonight.

"Have you had a massage before?" Mike whispered.

"Sure lots of times, but they doesn't qualify me as a masseuse.

Mike strapped the belt holding his massage oil around Chad's waist and looked at her imploringly. "Please, I have a daughter on the way and I need this job. I can't afford to get fired, not with a kid on the way. Please?"

Her anxiety spiked as she looked at Reagan's naked body lying on the table and then back at Mike. She hadn't touched a woman since Dawn, and she wasn't about to oil up this woman, run her hands up and down her naked body, and then have to take a cold shower afterwards.

"Please? I'll call Marsha and tell her to get a shake on it. She should be here in thirty minutes—tops. If you do her feet and hands, she'll be butter in yours. Use lots of oil, so you don't rub anything raw and don't rub too hard in any one area. If she's got a knot in a muscle you can just use the base of your palm and try and work it out. If it doesn't seem to give, move on to the next area. Oh, and just agree with anything she says. I do this for a living, trust me, they usually fall asleep before you get to their upper back."

"Oh god. Come on."

"Please, ma'am, this is my first child and I want to be there when she born. Surely, you've been there for someone when they needed you."

Chad felt a lump form in her throat remembering Dawn's last night. The night she wasn't there when she should have been. While this wasn't the same, it was just as important for him, and who was she to tell him not to be there when his wife needed him. Guilt worked her over like a boxer on a bag, and she knew she couldn't live with herself if she deprived him of one of the most important events ever.

"All right. Call Marsha and tell her to get a move on. I'll do the best I can."

"Thank you. My wife thanks you and my daughter thanks you."

"Go." Chad grabbed his arm and continued, "Out my door otherwise she'll know."

"Right. Thanks again." Mike hugged Chad and slipped out.

Before Chad could change her mind, she had washed her hands and was staring down at Reagan's feet. Trying to remember her last massage, she pumped the bottle several times, squirting oil everywhere, including her pants. Rubbing her hands together, she warmed up the oil and hesitantly grabbed one of Reagan's feet. Reagan let out a moan as soon as Chad touched it. Starting at the ball of her foot, Chad roughly rubbed her thumbs across the soft pad, up the arch and across Reagan's heel. The harder Chad rubbed the more Reagan moaned.

"God, that feels so good. I've had those damn heels on for twelve hours and my feet are killing me. I know they make men gaga, but I want to see a guy wear those all day and survive."

Chad agreed, women in heels made her gaga. The way they elongated the leg, the way her calves and ass tightened with each step, the swing of Reagan's

hip when she wore the stilettos sent a charge through
Chad. This would be so much easier without the
visuals, so Chad focused on the task at hand. Without
saying anything, Chad cradled Reagan's delicate foot
with one hand and pushed the heel of her palm across
the bottom. Her manipulations produced another deep
groan. Switching sides, she continued on the other foot,
again rewarded with the same low, almost orgasmic,
moans. Chad couldn't help but let her gaze roam up
the shapely leg. The towel covering her ass did little
to hide the rounded hump that topped her legs. She
pumped more oil in her hands and started to massage
Reagan's ankle before continuing up her calf. Working
her thumbs along the outer sides of Reagan's calf, she
could feel the tight, sinewy muscles gently give under
the pressure of her thumbs and palms.

Oh, God this is a bad idea, she thought as she
watched her hands work up and down the oiled,
muscular leg. Switching legs, Chad worked more oil
into her skin, trying to ignore the fact the massage was
starting to turn her on. Moving to the side of Reagan's
body, she slowly started to knead the tight thigh muscle
with both hands. Spreading oil over the long muscle,
she swept her hands from the back of the knee up to
the bottom of her ass. Accidentally, her pinkie brushed
the inside center of Reagan's cleft making her lift up
slightly.

Oh shit, shoot me now, God. Please. She squirmed
at the contact.

"If you weren't already married, and I was into
men, I might ask you to marry me, Mike. You have
wonderful hands," Reagan said, moaning again.

Chad's pulse hammered and it thrummed in her
warm hands each time she stroked Reagan's leg. When

she switched sides, Reagan spread her legs slightly, as if she were making room for the masseuse's hands. The shift only opened her center more to Chad's gaze. Mindlessly, Chad pumped furiously on the oil pump and squirting it on her slacks again. *Shit, I'm not going to get this out,* she thought, frowning at the wet spot on her zipper. She tried to refocus on her methodical kneading of Reagan's upper thigh, this time watching her hands to make sure she didn't touch something she shouldn't. More moans and longer strokes and Chad knew she had to move down to the base of the table, away from the temptation of another touch of Reagan's center. She placed a hand on each side of Reagan's thigh and pulled her fingertips firmly towards her ankle. Chad looked up each time she repeated the action, rewarded with a tantalizing peek at Reagan's naked ass. Switching legs, she performed the same operations again and took the same gratuitous glances.

"This might sound strange but could you massage my ass? I've been sitting all day and I think I carry all my stress there. Sounds weird huh?" The pillow muffled Reagan's voice.

Not strange at all. I make the same request when I get a massage.

Before Chad began, Reagan continued, "You've probably heard it all, but between you and me, the woman next door is just a pain in my ass, that's probably why I'm carrying it all there. God, she's such a bitch."

Chad knitted her eyebrows together and squinted at the defenseless woman. Flipping the towel in half she reached up and started to knead the tight muscle.

So, I'm a bitch, huh? she thought, oiling up her hands more.

"If it wasn't for the fact she's so damn easy on the

eyes, I'd have fired her a long time ago."

Oh really, does daddy know you call the shots?

"My father thinks very highly of her, so I guess I don't have a choice."

Trust me, if I wasn't doing this as a favor for a friend very high up, I'd fire myself.

"Oh that feels so good."

Of course it does. Chad smirked at the conversation in her head. *You should feel it from my side.*

"You probably hear all kinds of stuff from the people you work on don't you?"

You have no idea.

"I'm not usually this chatty, but for some reason I feel so comfortable. I guess that's what happens when you think this might be your last day on earth, huh?"

Hmmm, sounds serious. Chad said in her head.

"I think they call it an adrenaline high. It was the scariest thing I think I've ever been through."

If you don't follow orders I guarantee it won't be the last time you find yourself in danger. Death threats are something you take seriously in my line of work.

"Now, if I could only find a woman with your talents, I could be a happy, content woman." Reagan sighed and Chad felt her body relax under her touch.

Without thinking, Chad grabbed each cheek and pushed her ass up, and then ran her thumbs down the cleft of Reagan's ass. Chad felt her muscle pucker, but knew she was too polite to acknowledge the intimate touch. She continued to knead the taut ass muscle under her hand; this time though, Chad was thinking about what it would feel like to have Reagan's ass in her hands as she fucked her. A rhythmic pushing and pulling on the tight mound as she slid into Reagan's wet center.

Suddenly, she stilled her hands. Her heart beat so hard she swore Reagan could feel it through her fingertips as they glided across her skin. Looking down to where her watch usually was, she wished she knew how much time had passed. Surely, Marsha was going to arrive at any minute and save her from this awkward situation. She should never have agreed to give Reagan a massage. Now she was turned on and found herself thinking of all the ways she wanted to fuck her client.

"Your hands are magic, just magic, Mike." Reagan sounded tired.

In her lowest baritone, Chad answered. "Thanks."

"Could you get right between my shoulder blades? I have a knot that's been killing me. I get it every time I play tennis. I don't have much time for now, but I do try to squeeze in a game every now and then. Guess I take my frustrations out on a little green ball."

"Hmm."

"Oh, that's the spot. Yeah, right there. Oh, man. Yeah." Reagan moaned in delight.

A knock on the door in Chad's room jerked her hands to a stop.

"I'll get it," Chad said pushing Reagan's head back into the pillow before she could get a look at her masseuse.

"Thank god, you're here," Chad whispered pulling the replacement into her room.

"I got here as fast as I could. Sorry."

"No problem. She's in there," Chad took the belt off and handed the nearly empty bottle to Marsha. "She doesn't know I was the one doing the massage, so mum's the word."

"Okay." Marsha held up the bottle and then looked at Chad.

"Sorry, I guess I got a little carried away."

"I guess."

"Go, go before she figures out what's up."

"What should I tell her?"

"Just tell her Mike had to go, his wife was in labor, and you're here to replace him."

"Okay, works for me."

"Remember, she's not to know I was the one giving her the massage. It's our secret, besides there's a big tip in it for you if she doesn't find out."

"You got it."

Chapter Ten

Her body was reacting nicely to the strong hands working her muscles. If work was a drug, it was one she could easily wean herself off of, eventually. Everything that had happened that day seemed more like a nightmare rather than actual events. How could she have played right into Chad Morgan's hands? Chad had outsmarted her at every turn and she wasn't used to being outmaneuvered, at least not in business. It was still hard for her to believe someone was trying to kill her, other than the woman in the limousine. What was her name? Cheeta, Lita, no Rita? Not that it mattered. It was clear by Chad's reaction she had taken the routine too far.

The soft hands on her legs stopped with a knock on the door. All she could hear were a few whispered words and then a soft woman's voice addressed her.

"Good evening, Ms. Reynolds."

Reagan lifted her head up, shocked to see a tall woman standing next to her shoulders. She spied Chad leaning against the doorframe and directed her question to her bodyguard.

"What happened to Mike?"

Before Chad could answer, Marsha offered, "Oh, his wife just went into labor and he called me to come and finish working on you so he could be with her." Marsha oiled up her hands and spread them over Reagan's lower back. "I hope you don't mind. It's his first daughter and I'm sure you can appreciate him wanting to be there for his wife."

"Oh, of course." Reagan lowered her head back into the pillow and wished Mike hadn't left. He had been working magic on her body.

"He must have been doing a good job, your body is really relaxed."

"He was amazing, such strong hands."

"Well, I hope I don't disappoint, then."

Reagan let her mind wander as Marsha worked on her upper body. The knot coiled between her shoulders was stubborn and she felt Marsha knead the tight bunch until they finally released. Trying to breath through the pain, Reagan thought about Chad and wondered if the woman had ever had a massage in her life. She doubted she let anyone touch that tightly wound machine. Perhaps the woman in the picture could push all the right buttons on Chad to get her to relax. Thinking about the picture, Reagan couldn't help but notice her smile didn't reach her eyes. They were almost vacant in a lost sort of way. Without knowing why, she felt sorry for the woman and hoped she and Chad had more than what the picture showed.

"Okay, that does it for your backside. Would you like me to massage your front?"

"Um," Reagan hesitated for a moment. The thought of someone, a female, touching her body suddenly made her uncomfortable. The graze of thumbs across her anus and then the accidental touch of the masseuse's pinkie across her lips had nearly sent her through the table. Innocent enough, it was a reminder she hadn't been with a woman in months and her body could still react to a soft touch quite easily.

"No, not tonight, but I'll keep your card. It looks

as though I'm going to be here longer than I expected. Who knows? I'll probably need another one soon."

Raising herself up on her elbows, she realized Chad was still leaning in the doorway watching the exchange. Without thinking, Reagan sat up on the massage table letting the towel slip to the floor. If she expected Chad to blush at her exposed body, she was wrong. She watched Chad's eyes explore her body, finally resting on her full breasts.

"Like what you see?"

"Who wouldn't appreciate a beautiful woman?"

"Obviously you have no shame."

"Nope, if you're going to show it off, I'm going to enjoy it," Chad said in a husky tone that betrayed her. "Clearly, you have no shame, exposing yourself."

"If my memory is right, you've seen it all before anyway. So why claim false modesty?"

"Why indeed? Shall I help you get showered and dressed for dinner?"

Reagan noticed Chad's wet hair pulled back into a tight ponytail and the smell of fresh soap drifted into the room as she walked past her to talk to Marsha. Reagan couldn't help but notice how the shoulder holster pulled tight across Chad's bulk, framing her broad shoulders. The turtleneck fit like a second skin on Chad, hugging her pert breasts. Tucked into tight jeans Chad looked leaner than she did when wearing her blazer and slacks, which made her look bulkier, living up to her imposing body guard persona.

"Thank you, Ms. Reynolds. It's been a pleasure serving you. I hope your stay in De Moines is successful."

"Thank you, Marsha, I'm sure it will be. Good night."

"Nite."

As Marsha left with the table and bag, Chad called down to the kitchen to see about dinner. Confirming its arrival, she turned towards Reagan.

"Dinner should be here in about twenty minutes, just enough time for you to shower," Chad said, smiling. "Would you like me to wash your back?"

Reagan pulled the towel around her body and huffed, "You wish. By the way, I don't sleep with the hired help. In case you're wondering."

"Good to know we're on the same page."

"Same book, same page, same letter."

Reagan stalked out of the room before Chad let a smart-ass remark fly her way. She refused to let someone like Chad get under her skin again. She had put her through hell earlier and Reagan wasn't about to forget it, either. Turning the shower on, she let the room fill with steam. The warm, moist air clung to her, matting her hair and creating little dots of water on her oiled skin. She dabbed at a droplet of water pooled between her breasts, running the wet tip around her chest. A phantom game of connect the freckles created wet paths around her shoulders and chest before she dropped her towel and stepped into the shower. Relaxed muscles, melted further under the warm, pulsating jets of spray.

Her mind wandered to nothing, yet glimpses of the day's events flickered around her head like a grainy silent film. If she were honest, she had to admit she was more spooked than she realized. The shiny gun that had been pushed into her face filled her mind. She remembered how she'd felt, realizing there was no one to help her. She was all alone in the limo, with no escape from the situation without being hurt in the process. Trying to talk her way out of the limo wasn't going to happen. She could have easily been raped, beaten, or worse and no one knew her location. Not one person would have known where to find her, or if she had even arrived safely. Her own father, who had warned her, wouldn't know where she was until it was too late.

The pounding of the water echoed the pounding in her head as she pushed her palms firmly against her temples. She needed to stop obsessing about the day's events and move forward. She had to work with her security team. Turning control over to the arrogant woman would take everything she had, but deep down inside she knew it was necessary—if not for herself, at least for her father. Proving she could address any crisis head on was crucial now. Squeezing the water out of her hair, she stepped out of the shower and rubbed the towel roughly over her body. A light blush from the brisk contact of the towel covered her skin. Popping her contacts out, she rubbed her dry eyes and blinked at her reflection in the mirror. Tired, she looked tired, but it was nothing a good cocktail and a good night's sleep wouldn't fix.

✃✃✃✃

Reagan's retreat to her bathroom was a good thing because Chad wanted to slap her client. She wasn't violent unless it was warranted, and a smart-ass remark didn't constitute warranted. Reagan huffed into her bathroom and slammed the door, giving Chad a start. Surviving this assignment meant focusing more on the job and less on her client. There was only one goal on this mission and it was to keep Reagan

Reynolds alive until after Frank retired and the board voted her in as CEO.

"Two weeks, two long weeks," she whispered.

A sharp knock on the door caught Chad's attention. She pulled her pistol, and then looked through the peep hole. A man in a white hotel uniform, who seemed bored, stood beside a serving cart. Before he knocked again, Chad opened the door and stepped aside, allowing the waiter to enter.

"Don't leave yet," Chad said, lifting each cover off the plates arranged on the tray. Examining every inch of food, she replaced the tin covers and signed for the order. "Thank you. You can come back and get the tray in an hour."

"You can just leave it outside and we'll come by and pick it up."

"I've left you a big enough tip, I want you to come and pick-up the tray in exactly one hour. Do you understand?"

The waiter looked at the check and smiled. "You bet." Tapping his watch, he said, "8:55, exactly."

"8:55."

"Do you want to synchronize watches?" The waiter said with a smirk.

"That won't be necessary." Chad held the door, waiting for the waiter to leave.

"Would you like me to serve the dinner?"

"That won't be necessary."

"But for this tip, I'd—"

"No thanks," Chad said more forcefully. "One hour." Closing the door, she glanced around the room, moved a few pieces of furniture, and opened the French doors. She pushed the table closer to the open doors, taking advantage of the cool air, and arranged the plates. A final touch was to open the wine and turn off most of the lights.

Now this is more like it, she thought, smelling the inviting aromas. *Yeah, if your trying to seduce the woman.* Shit, this wasn't what she'd intended. Chad quickly moved to correct her error and turn on the lamps by the bed when Reagan walked out of the bathroom. *Great! Timing is everything.*

"What smells good?"

"Dinner is here."

"What are you doing?" Reagan asked, surveying the semi-dark room.

"I'm just turning on a light or two."

"Uh huh." Reagan raised an eyebrow at the explanation. "They were on when I went in to take my shower and now they're off."

"Yeah, well I was just checking the lighting. Making sure you could see things if you left the lights off, or at least almost off." Chad pulled a chair and motioned for Reagan to sit. Reagan pulled her robe tighter, then sat. Pouring a tasting of the wine, she took a sip then handed the glass to Reagan and waited before she filled the glass further.

"This is fine, thank you," she said placing the glass on the table.

"I'm glad you approve."

Pulling the covers from the dinner plates, Chad sat across from Reagan and waited for her client to start eating.

"Is this how you start your seduction, Ms. Morgan? A nice dinner, a bottle of wine, and mood lighting?" Reagan dipped a shrimp in the cocktail sauce and bit it, staring at Chad.

"Not usually. I'm more of a courting type of gal. I

like to pick a woman up at her house, meet her parents, and then go out on a date."

"Ah, the old fashion kind."

"Nothing wrong with that, is there, Ms. Reynolds?"

"I wouldn't know. I've never been courted, Ms. Morgan. I tend to prefer living in this century, where women can order their own food, drive cars and decide when or if they're going to sleep with their date."

"You're rushing it a bit don't you think? I hardly know you, and this isn't even a real dinner." Chad smiled at the innuendo.

"Well, aren't you the cute one?"

"As a matter of fact, I've been told I'm quite charming." Chad slapped at Reagan's hand as she reached for the last prawn, and then dipped it into the remaining cocktail sauce.

Feigning injury, Reagan waved her hand back and forth before wiping a dot of sauce from her fingers. "Yes, well I'm sure the girls at the Hoof and Paw Pub are easily impressed."

"Well, I'm sure in your circle of friends it would be considered funny, but it's just plan crass." Chad quirked an eyebrow and tilted her head to study Reagan. If she didn't know better, Chad would venture to guess this was Reagan's vain attempt at humor.

"And what would you know about crass, Ms. Morgan? Surely, you can't expect me to believe—"

"What, Ms. Reynolds? I might not have had the Ivy League education you've had, or the silver spoon shoved up my ass?" Chad watched Reagan eat as if she hadn't heard a word she'd said. "I went to college, just not the kind of prep school that made your parents name a building after them. No, I didn't graduate from the school of hard knocks as you might think. I went to a real college, joined the military and served my country for ten years before they retired me out. *Then* I went to the school of hard knocks," Chad said, chuckling to herself.

She had said too much as it was and she didn't owe this woman anything. She hated the way Reagan made her feel so defensive, as if she had done something wrong and should apologize.

"I see," Reagan said nonchalantly, spearing a vegetable off her plate.

The look she gave Chad could freeze fire, but Chad didn't intimidate easily, so she was going to have to do better than that. Pouring more wine into Reagan's glass and then her own, she sat back, rolling the stem between her thumb and fingers. Chad's skin burned and the cool breeze felt soothing. Her system was on overload after seeing Reagan naked earlier, and now she sat across from her, catching a glimpse of a partially exposed breast. If Reagan didn't know it was open, who was she to tell her? Hell, if she was going to be labeled crass, she was going to stare as long as she wanted and enjoy the view.

Chad studied Reagan's face and wondered why a nice looking woman like Reagan wasn't married. All the powerful, successful lesbians were doing it now; it was such a political statement. According to her plant on the plane, Reagan was enamored with children.

"So why did the military retire you out?" Reagan said as she wiped her mouth.

"I'm sorry?"

"Why did the military retire you?"

"Hmm, that's a little personal don't you think?"

"Why? I know you've delved into my background

and the background of those around me, so it's your turn." Reagan sat back, looked down, and discovered her open robe. Pulling it closed, she pursing her lips and threw another chilling glance at Chad.

"What?"

"Like what you saw?"

Chad shrugged her shoulders. "I've seen bigger."

"Really? I guess you're just a player, huh?"

"Not really, but women are all pretty much the same. Don't you think?" Chad surmised.

"What do you mean?"

"Legs, breasts, ass, and then there is their—"

"I get the picture."

"I thought you might."

"So, back to my question, why were you kicked out of the military?"

Chad smiled at the change in tactic. Kicked out of the military had a worse connotation that being retired out and Reagan knew it. It would take Reagan a few more mornings before she could compete against Chad in a game of words, but she was up to teaching the woman a lesson or two.

"I was a bad girl."

"Why am I not surprised?"

Chad shrugged her shoulders again and sipped her wine before looking at Reagan. "Because it takes one bad girl to know another, I suppose."

"You think..." Reagan's fingers touched her chest in feigned surprise before she continued, "I'm a bad girl. Give me a break."

"Now who's bullshitting who?"

"Clearly, you haven't done your homework."

"Really? What about the little fling in Tuscany

a few years ago? Fiorella what's-her-name, the Italian ambassador's daughter. I'm sure the little flower, or should I say *deflower*, is trying to salvage her reputation after she was found out just a month before her marriage. The press ate that one up. What about your little jaunt to the Swiss Alps with the singer, or perhaps you'd like to explain the cute little co-ed from your dorms who says she wasn't a lesbian until she met you? What's that saying, three drinks away from...anyway. So, who's calling whom a bad girl?"

Chad waited for a response, but when none was forthcoming, she looked up to see Reagan smugly sipping her wine. At least she could have the decency to blush at the accusations or even look embarrassed, but obviously, she was rather proud of her bad girl label. As long as she lived, Chad would never understand women, so why try?

"Ms. Italy, the ambassador's daughter, hit on me at an event held for my father. It wasn't my fault. I didn't speak Italian and she didn't speak English. I had no idea she was getting married and trust me, from what I read afterwards, she has her own line of cosmetics now thanks to all the press. As for the singer, well let's just say things aren't always as the press reports. She doesn't look any worse for wear to me. The college co-ed, we were both young. I gave it the ol' college try, but she turned me down. If she says otherwise, I'm fine with that. Besides in all of those events alcohol was a major contributing factor."

"Do you have a drinking problem I need to know about?" Chad asked, the slight concern evident in her voice.

"Not hardly. Besides, I didn't say I was drinking. I just said alcohol was involved."

"I see."

"Three drinks away...." Reagan purposely didn't finish the sentence.

"Hmm."

"Back to my question."

"Aw, yes. Why did they retire me?"

Chad took another sip of wine and set the glass on the table. She stood and leaned on the doorframe, looking out over the flat cornfields outside the window. Chad ran her fingers down her chest and abdomen feeling the scars underneath her shirt. How much did she want to divulge to someone who was just a client? Not much.

Chad turned when she heard a knock on the door.

"Expecting someone?" Reagan questioned.

"No, you?"

"Nope."

Chad pulled her sleeve back and checked her watch. It was too soon for the room service to pick up the tray. Chad peeked out the viewer and saw a young man holding roses. "Are you expecting a delivery?" Chad pulled her gun for the second time that night, stepped to the side and opened the door.

"Can I help you?"

"Delivery for Ms. Reynolds."

Chad looked at Reagan, who shrugged her shoulders and grabbed the flower vase from the young man. Snatching the flowers from Reagan, Chad asked the delivery boy, "Who sent these?"

"I have no idea, I'm just the messenger service. The florist told me some guy just said his wife was mad at him and we needed to deliver these ASAP to get him out of the dog house. He tacked on an extra fifty if I got it here tonight before five. There's a card." The kid pointed to one stuck in the middle of the bouquet.

"I think you have the wrong room, then."

The delivery boy looked at his clipboard and bunched his eyebrows together. "Isn't this Ms. Reynolds room?"

"Yep, but she isn't married. Unless I'm wrong," Chad said, looking at Reagan.

Reagan shook her head and shrugged her shoulders. "No, never been married."

"Okay, take 'em back."

"What? I can't. I have to deliver them."

"We don't want them."

"You have to take them."

"Nope."

"Shit. There's fifty in it for me if you take 'em."

"Sorry."

"Wait," Reagan said, grabbing Chad's arm. "Just let me smell them before you send them away. They're so beautiful." Before Chad could stop Reagan, she had her nose buried in the large bouquet, taking a deep breath. "Oh, they really don't smell do they?" Reagan moved her nose to another bunch of the flowers and inhaled again. "Hmm."

Reagan stood back up and then rocked slightly before she steadied herself on Chad's arm.

"Thanks," Chad said, hooking the door with her foot to slam it, but the delivery boy stopped it with his hand.

"What's that?" He pointed towards Reagan.

"What?" Chad was pissed the kid stopped the door.

"What's on her nose?"

Chad turned Reagan towards her. "Look at me."

A touch of white powder covered the tip and just under Reagan's nose. "Shit. Sit down. You," she said, pointing at the delivery boy. "Put those down and get me a wet wash cloth. Make sure it's dripping."

Chad sat a stunned Reagan on the couch. Seeing the powder, she was pissed at herself for not thinking about the possibility the flowers could be laced with something.

"What is it?" Reagan said.

"Don't touch anything. You have powder on your nose. Did you feel anything go up your nose when you smelled the flowers? Did it have an odor or did your nose tingle?"

"No, I guess I didn't notice anything."

Chad pulled the knife from her shoulder harness. She opened it and commanded, "Don't move. I want to get some of this powder off so I can have it analyzed." Gently, she scraped the blade across the top of Reagan's lip and the bottom of her nose, capturing some of the powder. Laying the knife on the coffee table, she turned her attention back to Reagan, whose eyes were starting to dilate.

"That's not good."

"What's not good?" Reagan tried to touch her nose.

"Don't touch." Chad pushed Reagan's hand down.

Drops of water caught her attention as the delivery boy shoved the washrag at Chad. "I gotta go."

Pulling her gun, she pointed it at the boy as she held the dripping cloth up to Reagan's nose.

"You try to leave and I'll shoot you. Now, get on the phone and call an ambulance, then call your boss. Now!"

"Okay, Okay."

"Reagan, we need to get you to the hospital. Then I'm going to call your father." Chad tried to sound as comforting as possible.

"No, don't call my father. He'll want me to stop what I'm doing. I have to make sure this transition is seamless or all of his hard work will be for nothing."

"I can't keep this from Frank. He has a right to know and he's my employer, not you. I'm sorry. I shouldn't have let you touch those flowers when I heard the shit story that kid told." Chad blamed herself for the situation, but she couldn't dwell on it now. She needed to get Reagan medical attention since it was possible the powder was poisonous.

"Okay, the ambulance is on its way and I've called my boss. He wants to know what happens immediately. Can I go now?"

"Not yet. Walk into that room over there," Chad said pointing to the open door. "My phone is on the dresser. Bring it here."

Chad gripped Reagan's hand and tried to comfort her, but her own nerves made it impossible, so she focused on the task at hand. First, get Reagan to the hospital. Next, get her team over here and start processing the room, and track down the scumbag who sent the flowers. The delivery boy tapped Chad on the shoulder and pushed the phone in her face.

"Hit the numbers one, three, and then hand me the phone." Chad placed her gun on her knee and grabbed the phone just as a male voice answered.

"Marcus, I need you to call Eric, Thomas, and Sophia back and then I need you to get up here. There's been an incident." Chad paused for a moment. "We're on our way to the hospital as soon as the ambulance gets here. I'll explain everything when you get here."

Slapping the phone closed, Chad tossed it on the table and looked at the kid sitting in the chair to her right. His pale complexion was only a tad darker than his white T-shirt and she noticed he was twisting his hat in his hands, probably to keep them from shaking.

"Where's your clipboard?"

"Over there." He pointed towards where he had set the flowers.

"Get it and bring it over here."

Taking the clipboard, Chad thumbed through the delivery receipts hoping to find some information on the person who sent the flowers.

"Is the credit card information on the receipt? I don't see anything here."

"We only have the last four digits. You'll have to get it from my boss."

"Call him back and make sure he knows what happened here. Tell him I want everything from this delivery, the phone number, the credit card information, the name of the person who sent these and I want it now. Do you understand me?" Chad's menacing tone clearly meant business.

"Yes, ma'am."

Chad heard the elevator bell ding, followed by the rattling wheels of a gurney being pushed toward her room. Looking back at Reagan, she couldn't help but feel sorry for her client. Her eyes were wide, but instead of looking like she was going into shock she seemed more relaxed, almost intoxicated. Hopefully, the hospital could counteract whatever poison the flowers had been dusted in.

"Someone called 911 requesting assistance?"

Chapter Eleven

Questions swirled around Reagan's head as the EMT, the hotel manager, someone she didn't know, and Chad all seemed to talk at the same time. She tried to watch as Chad answered all the questions with precision and efficiency. The way she dispatched the EMT, it seemed as if she had memorized Reagan's entire medical history. She heard the word poison and the room stopped moving, then as quick as it had stopped, everything suddenly shifted into high gear. She grimaced as a medic poked her left arm, establishing an IV line.

The hotel manager continued to wring his hands as he bombarded Chad with more questions. He informed Chad he must call the police and he had a duty to the other hotel guests. Within a few seconds, Chad was on the phone again, this time her tone was firm and ominous.

The board members. A few here were staying in the hotel, and if they saw Reagan taken out on a gurney, they would start to ask questions.

"The board members are here, Chad. I can't go to the hospital. They'll know something is wrong if they see me like this." Reagan felt like she was floating. Her head was foggy and she had a hard time focusing on anything in the room. Staring into Chad's eyes she felt like she smiled, hoping to reassure her bodyguard, but she couldn't be sure. Maybe it was all in her head, at least the part of her brain that was still able to reason with herself.

Chad refocused on the manager and informed him, "There will be a team here in a few minutes. They're going to sweep the room. If after they've done their job, you still feel you need to call the police after that, then be my guest."

Closing her eyes, Reagan suddenly realized her sinuses where burning. She felt a warm hand on her face and a soft whisper against her ear.

"Everything's going to be all right, just hang on, Ms. Reynolds. She's clammy, lets get her to the hospital," Chad said, her command left little room for an argument.

"I'll make sure the team gets in here and decontaminates everything," Marcus said rushing into the room. Clearly, he was assessing the situation as he bent down to study the roses. "Has anyone touched the card, Chad?"

"Not that I'm aware of." Chad looked at the delivery boy.

Tossing his hands up, he gingerly spoke, "It was in the bouquet when I picked it up."

"I'll get it bagged and checked when the crew gets here."

"When they get here I want you to get down to the hospital. I need to talk to the florist and question the delivery kid again. Just in case I missed something."

"You got it boss."

Chad looked at the bouquet. "Make sure you decontaminate it and check for prints and then I want to see it."

"You got it."

"We've got to go, ma'am."

Both EMTs stood, buckled Reagan in, and pulled the gurney up on its wheels. Reagan was having a hard time focusing on what was happening around her. In fact, she never felt more out of control than she did right now.

"Please don't leave me, I don't want to die alone," Reagan said, tears streaming down her face.

Chad wiped her tears and whispered in her ear. "Don't cry. I'm right here and I'm not going anywhere until you're stable. Okay?" To the EMTs she said, "Service elevator, not the main ones."

Reagan nodded and wiped away at the stream of tears that still fell. "Thanks."

A soft smile was her reward before they wheeled her from the room on her way to the hospital.

❧❧❧❧

"Marcus, don't overlook anything," Chad said, mentally reviewing a list of tasks to be finished before they returned. "Change hotels. Whoever sent those knew where we were, so let's get her out of here. Call me when you've got everything packed and I'll give you directions as soon as I have the new location picked out."

"You got it."

Chad snapped her pistol back in the holster and slipped her blazer on to cover the hardware she knew wouldn't be allowed in the hospital. She ran to the gurney just in time to make the elevator. Grasping Reagan's hand, she felt a tight squeeze. *How could I have missed the powder?* she chastised herself. She trained for any and everything and now only had herself to blame for Reagan's injury. Holding up the plastic bag that held the knife, she studied the white powder clinging to the blade. Someone found out where they were staying, but how? Chad had done an extensive background check on everyone associated with Reynolds Holdings. Someone had slipped through the cracks, but who? Racking her brain, she went through the dossier of employees who might have access to Frank and Reagan, but no one came to mind at the moment. She would pull all employee files when she got back to the location.

The ride to the hospital seemed to take forever, but it reality it was only five minutes from the hotel. The swish of the emergency room doors made Chad look up to see doctors running towards the ambulance.

"We got the phone call, what've we got?"

"Possible poisoning," Chad interrupted, lifting up the plastic bag displaying the knife. "I scraped some of the powder off her face. Can we get this analyzed as soon as possible?

"Nurse, take this over to the lab. We've got this from here," the doctor said, pushing Chad out of the way.

Chad pushed back. "I'm not going anywhere, so do what you have to do, but I'm not leaving her."

"Family?"

"Sorta."

"Oh," the doctor said as recognition flashed. "Well, we don't recognize same-sex relationships in the state, but we're sensitive to them at the hospital."

Chad's eyebrow quirked up, she wasn't going to correct him if it kept her close to Reagan. So she would let his wrong assumption stand.

"Good, I would hate to have to call my lawyer," Chad said playing along.

"That won't be necessary, just don't get in the

way."

"Chad?" Reagan said, weakly.

"Right here, honey."

"Where?"

Chad took Reagan's hand and walked next to the gurney as the doctor called for labs, blood work, and other assorted tests. Time seemed to drone on as she stood by watching Reagan get poked and prodded. The sweaty pallor of Reagan's skin worried Chad. Without knowing what the poison was, Chad had no way of knowing what to expect from Reagan. Would she start to convulse in reaction to the poison, would her body start to stiffen and arch, or would she just fade away? Chad's mind went through all the possible side effects of poisoning. Ricin, Arsenic, Mercury and the list went on and on, each with their own deadly consequences.

"Can I see you outside?" The doctor tapped Chad on the shoulder and motioned to the door.

"I'll be right back. Don't go anywhere without me, okay?"

"I'll try not to."

"That a girl. Chin up, it'll be okay." Chad pulled the door closed; she didn't want Reagan hearing the possible bad news. "How bad is it Doc?"

"Actually, not bad at all, she was poisoned—sort of, but whoever did this mixed cocaine with a tiny bit of talcum powder. Diluted, but still pretty potent stuff. There's enough in there to screw with her. Minor stuff really, her sinuses are inflamed and bleeding, but she won't have any lasting damage. We've flushed her sinuses, gave her a drug to counteract the cocaine, so I think we've gotten everything out. The wet washrag you applied right after the incident was a great idea. Some of the water went into her nose and washed part of the mucus membrane."

"Thank god."

"Any idea how this happened?"

"Yes, but we're letting the police handle it," Chad lied, but the doctor didn't need to know. Someone would be by to talk to him so it would look official and hopefully, wouldn't raise any suspicions. If it did, she would deal with it later. Reagan was safe and that was all that was important.

"Thank you," Chad said, extending her hand. "I can't thank you enough for saving her life."

"No problem, it's my job. I'm just glad this has a happy ending."

"Me, too."

"You'll be able to take your girlfriend home, in about a couple of hours. I just want to make sure there aren't any residual side effects."

"Thanks, Doc."

"You're welcome."

Chad waited until the doctor was far enough away before she pulled out her phone and texted Marcus. Waiting, she finally heard the return beep of Marcus's text. He would be there within the hour and she would be able to leave Reagan long enough to try to find out who had sent the roses.

Stepping back into the room, Chad quietly closed the door and stood back, staring at Reagan. She lay on the bed, curled inward. Her slow shallow breaths barely moved her chest and Chad worried the effects of the cocaine might be more serious that she thought, but the doctor had assured her Reagan would recover. As she sat on the stool next to the bed, Chad reached for her small hand and ran a finger over Reagan's knuckles where her hand gripped the rail. With her eyes closed she looked at peace, but Chad new directly under that façade was a she-devil waiting to be released. For now though, Chad would enjoy this side of her client. Soon enough things would be back to normal and she would spend her days and probably nights, again wondering why she had taken the job.

"What did the doctor say?"

Chad looked into Reagan's soft, sleepy eyes as they gazed back at her. The start of a smile broke across Reagan's face as Chad smoothed the back of her hand.

"You're going to be fine in a few days. Luckily the cocaine was mixed with talcum, diluting it potency."

"What? Really?" Reagan's voice chilled.

"Yes, I'm afraid so. You're father had every right to be worried for your safety. Now perhaps you'll take things more seriously, Ms. Reynolds."

"Yes, I suppose I've been reckless, haven't I?" Her tone was low and apologetic.

Chad felt sorry for Reagan, all alone, facing a threat that almost succeeded. She knew a woman like Reagan probably wasn't use to depending on others for help. It was lonely at the top of the corporate world in general, but a woman faced an even lonelier existence, rarely finding anyone who could understand the self-imposed isolation. Add to that a woman whose mother died in childbirth, which no doubt carried a lot of baggage, and Chad wondered how it affected her view of the world, not to mention her place in it. Self-sufficient, angry, determined, and independent; all ideas that came to mind when she thought about Reagan. Chad suspected now Reagan had to come to terms with the fact that she'd need to depend on someone, and there was actually a death threat looming over her head.

Chad's jobs often had her staring death in the

face. In fact, she still bore the scars of one attempt on her own life, and this made her more suited to handle threats of this kind. Someone like Reagan, who worried more about her latest footwear choices, was less suited to deal with adversity than most. Perhaps now Reagan would listen to her and do what was necessary to keep herself safe. That would lighten Chad's load just a little. The silence between them passed a few moments more before Chad finally answered her question.

"I'm sure you see the gravity of the situation. I'm only sorry I didn't do my duty and protect you, as I should have. I hold myself personally responsible for tonight. You can be sure it won't happen again." Chad stood and pulled the blanket tighter around Reagan. She had seen Marcus peek his head in the door, ready to relieve her. "I'm afraid I'm going to have to leave you for a while, Reagan," she said, nodding her head towards the door. "I've arranged for some meat to hang around your neck. Marcus is one of my most trusted employees. I trust him with my life."

"I can't go back to the hotel, Ms. Morgan. Whoever sent those flower knew where we were," Reagan pleaded.

"I've made other arrangements. No one knows where we're staying. I'll call your father and let him know what's happened."

"No!" Reagan sat up, clutching her head. "If he finds out he'll make me come home and the board will put someone else in his place."

"Your father retains the voting majority, so that's impossible."

"Yes, but the board expects to see strong leadership. They need to have confidence in the transition. Otherwise, we could lose our military contracts. They're worth millions to the company. Too many families depend on us, so I have to do this, period."

Chad worried about Reagan. Her self-imposed mission to represent a strong, competent head of Reynolds Holdings would drive her forward, but perhaps she was missing the bigger picture, her own life. If things escalated and someone was trying to kill Reagan, Reynolds Holding would be at the mercy of the board anyway. Chad would try explaining that later. Her immediate priority was tracking down who had sent the flowers and eliminating the threat. Marcus stood at the door waiting for permission to enter farther. Carrying a bag, he lifted it with a shake and raised his eyebrows.

"Come in, Marcus." Chad reached for the bag and checked inside.

"I noticed Ms. Reynolds only had a robe on, so I brought some clothes for her when she checks out. There's a set in there for you, too. I think you should change what your wearing as well, Chad."

"Good idea. I was so busy I completely forgot about our clothes. Thanks, buddy." Chad turned towards Reagan, who was now sitting up and pulling the blanket up to her chin. "Ms. Reynolds, may I introduce my partner, Marcus?"

"Ms. Reynolds."

"Mr. Marcus."

"Just Marcus, ma'am."

"Okay, Just-Marcus."

"Well, at least you still have your sense of humor through all of this," Chad said, laying some clothes on the bed.

"Yes, well that might be short-lived if I'm not

careful."

"You'll be careful from now on, I'm sure of it," Chad reassured her. "Any word from the gals?"

"Not yet, but they're working on the room."

"Ms. Reynolds, I have to start my investigation to identify who's responsible for this, so I'm going to take off. Marcus will be here if you need anything."

"I understand."

"Please don't speak to anyone right now. We don't know how they learned where we were staying. Until I can figure this out, it's best not to call anyone."

"Not even my father?"

"Not even Mr. Reynolds. Not yet."

Chad knew she should call Frank, but Reagan was right, he would pull the plug on everything. While that would keep Reagan safe, it wouldn't help Chad find the stalker. She needed time to flush him out and she needed to formulate a plan of attack rather than play defense at this point.

"Marcus, she should be released in a few hours. Take her to the safe house and I'll meet you there later. I'll explain things to the doctor. When the ladies are done I'll send them over to relieve you."

"Please don't send the woman from earlier. I don't want her anywhere near me." Reagan sounded scared now. The attempted poisoning had added to an already stressful day, and that was putting it lightly.

"No problem, I'll make sure Rita is put back in her cage," Chad said, hoping she sounded apologetic. "I'll see you later, Ms. Reynolds. Please don't worry, we're going to catch this asshole if it's the last thing I do."

"Your clothes?"

"I'll bag them up. I need to get going. I'll see you

later."

"Thank you Ms. Morgan. I appreciate your quick thinking. The doctor said it made all the difference."

Chad saw the rough edges soften a little as Reagan pouted and pursed her lips. Yep, this duty was going to be tougher than she'd expected.

Chapter Twelve

Lonely was a feeling Reagan was accustomed to; she was alone from the minute she was born. Her father had done everything he could as fathers do for their daughters, but she missed out on the motherly influence that made women soft and comforting. The world of women was only something she had seen in college. The way girls talked, the way they interacted, the way they comforted each other when things were bad. She had grown a hard shell to get through life. In fact, she had developed sharp instincts and rough edges, competing in a man's world, and mostly they served her well. This time she needed something, someone to hold her, to comfort her and tell her everything was going to be all right. If Reagan had a best friend, she assumed she would be the first person she would call. She didn't have a best friend, though.

Studying Marcus, she watched him texting someone and smiling. Probably his wife, she thought. People did that, she noticed, texting and smiling. How could they smile when the world was in such a shitty state? How could they be so oblivious to the cruel things happening around them, the dog-eat-dog world chewed you up and spit you out if you weren't careful? Fools, they were all fools.

"Would you mind if I got dressed?"

"Not at all," Marcus said, handing her the stack of clothes he'd brought. "I just reached into your bag and grabbed stuff that looked like it went together. Sweats and shoes. I hope it was all right?" Reagan arched an eyebrow at him. "I didn't look at anything else you might have had in there. Promise," he said, crossing his heart.

"I appreciate you bringing me something to wear. That was very considerate of you."

"No problem."

"Do you mind stepping out so I could change?"

"Sorry, but Chad left explicit instruction not to leave you alone."

"And you follow her instruction to the letter."

"To the letter, ma'am."

"Well, can we at least pull the curtain so I can have some privacy?"

Marcus's gaze darted around the room, from the window, to the tray of supplies, then to the door.

"Don't worry, I'm not looking to escape or kill myself, if that's what you're worried about."

"No, ma'am. I'm just checking to make sure there isn't another way into the room. That's all."

She waited until Marcus closed the curtain before slipping off the flimsy hospital gown. The light-headed feeling every time she stood up hampered the dressing process.

"So tell me about Ms. Morgan," she said, trying to ignore the spinning room.

"I'm sorry?"

"Tell me a little about your boss. She hasn't really been very talkative and I like to know a little about the people who work for me."

"Those are things she should tell you, ma'am."

The good employee, she thought. Chad would undoubtedly chastise anyone who divulged personal information about her. Marcus had likely been told on day one what happens within the company, stays within the company, including any information about personnel. She decided to try a different tactic.

"Okay, well tell me about yourself then. I saw you smiling when you were texting. Are you married, do you have kids?"

"Ma'am that probably isn't important right now."

"If we're going to be spending the next couple of weeks together in close quarters, I'd like to be able to hold a conversation with you, but I understand if your boss is a hard-ass. I wouldn't want to get you in trouble," she said, throwing the bait into the water.

"She's not a hard-ass at all. She really a great gal."

He'd taken the bait. Now, she simply had to set the hook and reel him in.

"I'm sorry, all I've seen is the hard-ass side of Ms. Morgan. I'm sure she's a good boss."

"She is. I've known her since the military, so I speak from experience. Just don't get on her bad side. Don't make her an enemy and you'll be fine."

"She has a temper, huh?"

"Not a temper, no, but she's good at what she does and takes her job seriously. I'd want her protecting my family," Marcus confided.

"Boys or girls?"

"Two girls. They're the love of my life."

"I love kids. Doubt I'll have any, but I love them."

"So I hear."

"News travels fast, I see," Reagan said, sliding the curtain back.

"We're a team and we plan these things out to the smallest detail."

"Well, I guess Ms. Morgan didn't plan on this happening did she?" Her tone was almost accusatory, but she couldn't help it. She immediately wished she hadn't said it.

"Trust me, she's beating herself up over tonight, don't worry." Marcus's back stiffened as he locked eyes with her. "You should probably rest, now. If you want more information you'll have to ask Chad yourself."

"My apologies if I was out of line," Reagan said, trying to crawfish out of this situation.

"No apologies necessary. Besides, I know when I'm being played, Ms. Reynolds, so you'll have to do better. By the way, I don't have any children." Marcus smiled.

She'd been beaten at her own game.

⊰ℬℬℬ⊱

Chad had been driving around De Moines for the past fifteen minutes to ensure she wasn't followed. Doubling back, she finally pulled into the driveway of the house, killed her lights, and looked around the deserted middle class neighborhood. So far, she'd had to call in one too many favors to keep Reagan Reynolds safe. At this rate, the agency was going to get her next protection detail free, or worse she would have to take a black ops mission. Pulling her bag from the car, she hurried to the door and knocked softly.

The metallic sound of the sliding deadbolt brought her attention back from wandering around the neighborhood. The door cracked open with the chain firmly in place until her identification was confirmed.

The door shut quickly and the chain slid, scraping the door before it swung just wide enough to allow her entrance to the darkened room.

"What took you so long? I was starting to get worried." Marcus flicked on the living room light. Laid out on the floor was an arsenal of weapons in various states of breakdown for cleaning.

"Expecting company?" Chad said, pointing to the hardware.

"Nope. Just bored."

"Where's Sophia?"

"In there with Ms. Reynolds."

"Is there a problem?"

"Nope. I just didn't want her to be alone after what happened tonight." Marcus turned back to his work. "The doctor gave her something for her nerves and she was out like a light. In fact, I had to carry her in she was so out of it."

"You're such a softy."

"I am not."

"Are to."

"Am not."

"Fine, have it your way. Why aren't you in bed?" Chad questioned, knowing Marcus only cleaned the equipment when he was nervous.

"I was just thinking about what happened tonight. Did you find anything out from the florist?"

"Not much. He said the order was placed back in California. The kid was kind of talking out of his ass."

"How so?"

"Well…" Chad tossed her jacket on the back of a chair and flopped down on the sofa. She was exhausted, but she knew it would be hours before she could catch any sleep. "The order was placed online. Whoever ordered it paid extra and put a rush on it. They filled out the comments section on the order, saying it was 'for his wife, with whom he had a fight with earlier in the day', and asked the florist to put a rush on it so she would get it before going to bed."

"That's all it took?"

"Yep. The florist said it all seemed legit. He got a call from a guy inquiring about the order." Shaking her head, she continued, "Before you go there, De Moines has over twenty florists who take orders online, so whoever placed the order called the online company to find out whom they dealt with in De Moines. I called about the credit card. It's one of those pre-paid cards available at any grocery store. Same thing with the phone, they're simple to buy at a convenience store. The kind drug dealers use—untraceable. Whoever is after Reagan Reynolds wants her dead and they're either a pro or is paying a professional."

"Or just damn lucky."

"Why do you say that?"

"How many people knew she was at that hotel?"

"You, me and the team, and her father. No one else."

"Maybe the father said something to someone?"

"We've checked everyone with the company. We've checked those closest to Reagan and Frank, then widened the circle and checked out everyone closest to them."

Marcus walked to the table and grabbed the plastic zip bag with the card from the flowers inside. He handed it to Chad. "It's clean. No fingerprints, no licking the envelope, so we won't get a DNA match, but you should read the inside. Someone's been watching too many movies."

Chad opened the envelope and slid the card out, rotating it, examining the front and then the back. The card could be purchased in any drug store, supermarket, or card shop. Nothing stood out about the card. The front showed a silhouetted couple walking on the beach with the setting sun. The typical, sappy "I love you" written across the front in gold writing. She thumbed the corner and opened the card. Letters cut out from a newspaper were glued on the inside. Chad read the text out loud, "U might run, but U can't hide. Ur dead bitch." She raised an eyebrow quizzically at Marcus. "The letter U instead of you, and Ur instead of you're. Conservation of letters?"

"I think they needed space to fit all of it on the card. All bold face letters from the headline of a newspaper. We can't trace the newsprint. I ran a sample of the paper and the glue used. It's a standard glue stick and the same newsprint used by tons of newspapers."

"No prints anywhere?"

"Probably used latex gloves."

"Great," Chad said, putting the card back in the envelope and sealing it in the zip bag. Tossing it on the table, Chad sat on the sofa and scrubbed her face.

"Okay, so what's next?" Marcus asked.

"Maybe she's bugged. If we're the only people who knew, how did someone find out where she was?"

"Not possible. I took everything out of her luggage. By the way, she's got a few little toys in the bag, but you didn't hear it from me," he said, smiling. "I ran the bug zapper over her luggage, her clothes, her briefcase and she's squeaky clean."

Letting out a sigh, Chad dropped her head against the sofa. What was she missing? Something was out of place, but she couldn't quite put her finger on it. Call it a feeling, but she knew she had overlooked something.

"I'm going to relieve Sophia. Try to get some sleep. Reagan has a lunch appointment with a board member tomorrow and I'll need at least one of you with us. Where's Rita?"

Glancing down at his watch, Marcus said, "I sent her home after we decontaminated the hotel room. I figured she should start running down leads back in California, and after what happened yesterday, she was the last person Ms. Reynolds needed to see."

Chad nodded her head in agreement. Marcus could read a situation as well as she could and she trusted his judgment. Out of sight meant out of mind, and if Rita wanted to keep her job, she needed to be as far away from the situation she had created as possible.

"By the way, Ms. Reynolds was quizzing me about you tonight."

"Really?"

"Yeah, I think she thought she had me, but she's a rank amateur when it comes to getting intel. I had her thinking I had kids and she had an ally."

"Hmm."

"Don't worry, I told her if she wanted to know anything, she'd have to talk to you."

"Oh, and I'm sure she will."

Marcus laughed, "I'm sure she will, too." Chad stood, yawned, and then stretched. "Want me to take your shift?"

"Naw, I'm good. Which way to her bedroom?"

After a quick tour of the house, Marcus and Chad parted ways, each going to their respective jobs. Chad quietly opened the door, glad it didn't squeak when she pushed on it. Sophia jumped to her feet, reaching under her windbreaker for her weapon.

"Hey, hey, it's just me." Chad held her hands up, but stayed rooted at the door, making sure Sophia was clear who had opened it.

"Sorry, Chad," she said. Motioning Chad outside, she leaned in and whispered. "I can sit with her if you want to get some sleep."

"Naw, I'm good. If I get tired, I'll just sleep in the chair. If she freaks out in the middle of the night, I want to make sure someone is there to calm her down. It isn't every day someone tries to kill you and I don't know how she's going to handle it all when it finally sets in."

"I don't think she's going to wake up. Marcus said the doctor gave her something for her nerves and she hasn't moved since I went in."

"Good, maybe I can get some sleep then."

"You sure?"

"I'm good, thanks. Get some sleep. We start fresh in the morning."

"In the morning then."

"In the morning," Chad echoed, walking into the bedroom. As she closed the door, she looked around the room, noting where everything was. The last thing she wanted was to fall face first over something and wake Reagan. Spying the chair Sophia had just vacated, Chad sat, pulled her gun, and set it on the arm. She slipped her harness and rolled it up, placed it on the dresser, and flexed her shoulders. Although it felt like part of her anatomy, losing the weight of the gun felt good.

Chad pushed the chair closer to Reagan's bed so she could see her better. The off camber location of the chair gave her a less than ideal view of the sleeping woman, and she wanted to keep eye contact on her at all times, even if there wasn't an immediate threat. She had screwed up tonight and had only herself to blame.

That kind of mistake wouldn't happen again. It had cost her dearly once, and tonight it almost looked like it would happen again, but not if Chad had anything to say about it.

Sliding down into the soft cushions of the chair, Chad ran her fingers through her hair massaging her scalp. Her body felt like a spring wound too tightly. Her muscles ached and her neck stretched slightly as she rotated her head trying to loosen the tension. Pushing her chin, she felt a loud pop and worried it might wake Reagan. Reagan had curled up in a tight ball in the center of the king-size bed, clutching one of the pillows. She seemed almost child-like; the way one hugged a favorite stuffed animal, dwarfed in the huge bed. Her breathing was slow, methodical, and relaxed. Looking at her, no one would guess she could have lost her life earlier just from the simple act of smelling flowers.

Chad let a deep sigh escape, a habit she was trying to break. It seemed her team mistook the action for displeasure, and she didn't want to send the wrong message if she could help it. Right now though, it seemed acceptable, considering everything she had been through. From the crap at the airport, to a visit to the emergency room, so far nothing was going to according to the plan she had painstakingly laid out. The only highlight to the day, if there was one, was the massage she had given Reagan. Closing her eyes, she remembered the feel of the soft, pliant skin. The way Reagan's muscles relaxed under her touch sent a spear of warmth through Chad's body. It had been months since she'd placed her hands on another woman's body and the innocent touches across Reagan's made her wish she had more time to devote to a partner. She would have to be happy with the occasional one-night stands she found herself searching out. She didn't consider these types of encounters intimate. Pay for play, in Chad's mind wasn't touching, sharing, or even reciprocating. She never touched them and it was purely selfish on her part. They didn't come with long-term contracts, and rarely demanded more than a gut wrenching orgasm as payment.

Studying the innocent face that now rested, Chad smiled, remembering the night she met Reagan. The self-assured way she'd fought Chad that night was appealing, or maybe it was the way her breast played peek-a-boo. The firm, taut ass pressed against Chad practically had her unhinged. The more Reagan fought, the harder her ass pressed against Chad, sending a spike of excitement through her. Tonight though, she looked like she needed a protector, someone who would vanquish the monster hiding under the bed. Reagan's tousled and messy brown hair framed her face and her lips pouted as if recently reprimanded, but what Chad couldn't stop thinking about that beautiful body she had her hands all over tonight. The way the oil gave it a slick sheen accenting the muscles in her legs and ass. The way Reagan moaned through the whole ordeal, made Chad want to turn her over and pleasure the woman, but she didn't dare. Crossing the lines between employee and employer was a big no-no in her mind, but it didn't stop her from fantasizing about the sexy body sprawled out before her tonight.

Reagan groaned and jerked on the bed, instantly bringing Chad to her feet. Standing at the foot of the king size bed, she loomed over Reagan as she thrashed side to side. When it didn't stop, Chad kneeled on the bed and gently placed her hand on Reagan's arm trying to still her. While the movements slowed, they didn't stop completely, so Chad gently whispered close to her head.

"Shh, it's okay. You're going to be fine. Shh, shh."

As quickly as it started, it ended, leaving Chad's hand on Reagan's arm. Sitting back down, she watched Reagan closely, waiting for the nightmare to resurface. Anger at herself returned. How could I have been so stupid? she wondered. There would be no more mistakes on this job, none. She wouldn't forgive herself if something happened to a client.

"How long have you been here?" Reagan asked, her voice heavy with sleep.

"Not long."

"You should get to bed. It's been a long day for both of us."

"I will, don't worry. I just want to make sure you're all right."

"Thanks," Reagan offered.

"For what?"

"For saving my life."

"Yeah, well..."

"No, yeah well's, your quick thinking stopped a bad situation from getting worse. Who knows, I probably would have kept trying to smell all of those roses and then I would have been really screwed."

"Do you do that all the time?"

"Do what?"

"Stop and smell the flowers."

"Probably not after today, but I used to, yes. I love flowers. Their simple, elegant beauty. They make me smile and yet they just grow, simple, easy, and no strings attached beauty."

"Well, I should let you get back sleep." Chad

stood to leave.

"Wait."

They watched each other for long moments. Staring at Reagan in the silence made Chad slightly uncomfortable, so she looked around the room.

"Is there something else you needed?"

"Um," Reagan sat up and swept locks of hair out of her face. "Maybe you could stay a bit longer?"

Chad heard desperation in Reagan's voice and it broke her heart. She was sure it took everything she had to ask and Chad wanted to respect what Reagan had just gone through, not minimize it. "Sure."

Reagan scooted farther away from the edge and patted the bed next to her. Without a word, she gazed up at Chad imploringly with a half-hearted smile.

"I just don't want to be alone right now."

A quick nod was all Chad could manage; words seemed to leave her at that moment, watching Reagan patting the bed. Looking back at the door and then the bed, Chad's feet felt glued to the floor. Fear had suddenly paralyzed her. Her earlier sexual thoughts of Reagan only added to her anxiety. Faced with sitting in bed with a beautiful woman, who just happened to be her client as well, made her hesitate.

"I'm not sure it's a good idea, Ms. Reynolds."

"Really, I don't bite and I'm the boss, remember?" Reagan patted the bed again.

"Actually, your father's the boss, Ms. Reynolds," Chad reminded Reagan, hoping it would cool her down.

Nodding, Reagan sighed. "I just don't want to be alone, but I understand you want to keep this professional. Now, if you'll excuse me, I need to try getting some sleep. I expect it will take me a while after tonight's events." If Reagan was trying to guilt her, it was working.

"Slide over," Chad said, sitting on the edge of the bed.

Instead of sliding over, Reagan slid towards the center, not away from Chad. Chad cleared her throat and leaned back against the headboard, one foot still on the floor.

"That can't be comfortable," Reagan said, scooting down farther.

"I'll be fine," Chad assured her.

"Lie down. If you fall asleep I promise to behave." The smirk Reagan tossed her didn't instill confidence in Chad. "Look, I'll even sleep with my back to you, if it makes you feel any better."

Chad slid down farther onto the bed and smacked at a pillow Reagan handed her. She punched it up to align her head so she could see the door. The bed dipped as Reagan moved even closer, making contact and curling her butt against Chad's hip. Pulling the covers over Reagan, Chad tucked them tightly between their bodies, trying to make sure they weren't touching. Something compelled her to comfort Reagan, and she rubbed her hand along her upper arm.

Before long, she heard Reagan's soft snores as she fell quickly asleep. Chad relaxed, taking in the body resting next to hers, knowing she could easily sleep with the woman lying with her, and that wasn't a good thing.

Chapter Thirteen

The towel hung off Chad's hips as she finger combed her hair. The stress of the job was taking its toll, but worse, she felt as if she was sinking in quicksand every time she was around Reagan. It was clear Reagan wasn't respecting her boundaries; therefore, she would find a way to make her respect them. She needed to rebuild the walls she had set firmly in place when Dawn died, if not, she would compromise the job. Water drops flung everywhere as she wiped her hand down her chest. She traced her finger across a one-inch scar and then another and another. She had grown so used to them that she no longer saw them anymore. They were a part of her that went unnoticed—except one—the longest scar that ran down the center of her abs stopping at her navel. The blade had nearly sliced her open when it had happened and the doctors were surprised she had survived, despite the viciousness of the attack. Nevertheless, it was just another piece of luggage she carted around and rarely opened, because no one saw her naked.

"Oh my!"

"What the fuck?" Chad grabbed her breasts.

"I knocked, but I guess you didn't hear me." Chad watched Reagan's eyes travel from scar to scar and then follow the long one, only looking up when she reached the end. "How did you get those?" Reagan stepped towards Chad with a hand out as if to touch her scars. Chad stepped back out of reach, putting a hand out to stop her touch.

"If you don't mind, Ms. Reynolds. Please."

"Oh, I'm sorry I don't know what I was thinking." Reagan turned her back to Chad. "I need to be zipped."

If Reagan's intrusion didn't piss her off, her arrogance did, demanding to be zipped as if she had just asked Chad to pass the butter at dinner. Chad sighed and stepped just close enough to zip the tight dress. When she looked at her semi-naked back, Chad couldn't help noticing Reagan wore no slip, giving Chad ample time to check out the matching panties that looked more like something to seduce a lover than something a business professional would wear. The thought of slipping the lace thong off the tight, round ass sent a shiver slicing right through her. If the massage hadn't done enough to send her over the edge, spiraling into the endless daydream of sex with her employer, the vision of Reagan sitting there in the lace naughties would seal the dream.

Shaking herself back into the moment, she zipped the snug black dress, then stepped back and covered herself. Now, remembering she stood damn near naked in front of her boss, she was just past embarrassed, moving quickly to annoyance. The lack of an invitation didn't seem to bother Reagan as she turned, taking one last look at Chad, her eyes once again searching her scarred body. *If this is the start of the day, it was going to be a humdinger,* Chad thought shaking her head.

"I'll be waiting for you in the front room. Sorry, I should have knocked harder."

"I'll be ready in about ten minutes. Why don't

you make sure you've eaten, I don't want you getting sick today."

"Right. Would you like some coffee and toast? I went ahead and asked Sophia if she could fix some for us. I hope it was all right?"

"I'm sure she's thrilled to be asked to make coffee. I hope you were nice about it."

"Of course. In fact, I started to rummage through the cabinets for the coffee maker, but she shooed me out, saying she would take care of things. Something about she knew how you liked your coffee and toast." Reagan shrugged, still standing in front of Chad, staring at her long scar.

Chad recognized the visceral reaction to her vicious scars when Reagan shivered. The women she had been with never saw her in the light. She made it a point to keep the room dark and make them leave before morning. Paying a woman allowed you to make the rules and she had no problem paying for pleasure. If they did see the scars or feel them during sex, they had the decency to never ask about them, money had a way of keeping mouths shut. The scars were the reason she never tried to date a woman. They were hideous and if Reagan's reaction was any indication, they were still very noticeable.

"Do you mind, or would you rather stand there and watch me get dressed? You are the boss, as you say, so if you're not going to leave," Chad said, dropping the towel and turning towards the chair with her slacks slung over it.

"I'm gone, I'm gone."

Reagan slammed the door as she left, but not before popping her head back in. "Sorry. I didn't mean to slam it."

Chad's smug smile clearly freaked Reagan out because she slammed the door once more. She heard a muffed *sorry* through the door and chuckled. It was definitely going to be one of those days. She wanted to remind Reagan of the ground rules concerning privacy and boundaries. Having seen her scars would make the discussion easier, she just didn't want to see the pity-look when someone saw her scarred up body. The road maps, as she thought of them, of her past life made her feel ugly, damaged, and unworthy, especially since she felt she had little to offer any woman who got involved with her.

She clenched her fists, thinking about how she got the damn things. It angered her every time she thought about him and hoped he was enjoying his government's accommodation. It was the least the government could do for putting him on her team. The agent had tried to get her drunk and into bed. When she resisted his advances, and threatened to have him kicked from the assignment, he surprised her when he pulled the knife he wore on his belt and started stabbing her. Even in his drunken state, he managed to stab her six times before she fell to the ground. Thinking he had killed her, he gave her a kick to the face, breaking her jaw. At first it was her word against his, her hot temper only added validity to his story. The scratches on his neck were his undoing. Lucky for her, the doctor at the hospital had clipped her nails, thinking she might have been raped, too. Trying to control her temper, she opened her hands, took a deep breath and worked to clear her mind of the incident. Finally, she could refer to it as an incident and not attempted murder, but it had taken years to get to this place. Her fingers slid down the long surgical scar, left behind when the doctors saved her life. It seemed pointless to dwell on what was done. The past followed her around, ready to be rediscovered, all she had to do was look at her body. *Enough*, she thought. *I've wasted enough time today on this pity party, move on.*

Grabbing her shoulder harness, she slipped it on, adjusted its position on her body, and then pulled her blazer on. The weight of the iron she wore gave her comfort when little else did. She knew she could count on it, knew its limitations, and how to compensate for them. Women, now that was a different story.

❦❦❦❦❦

Reagan rushed to her bathroom and grabbed the sink for support. Scars. Reagan had never seen something so violent in her life and violent was the only word to describe the purplish marks on Chad's chest. The worst one ran the length of the lean torso, dead center of her body. Squeezing her eyes closed as if she could banish the images from her memory, she felt embarrassed for barging into her bodyguard's room without knocking. She didn't know why she had done it. With Chad lying next to her last night, she wanted nothing more than to run her hands over the warm body cradling hers. Feeling Chad's strong arms wrapped around her made her feel safe, protected, and interestingly enough, cared for. She knew it was all in her mind, but it had been so long since she had felt that way. It was almost a foreign feeling—almost.

Looking past her reflection in the mirror, she still couldn't erase the ravages of Chad's body from her mind. Had Chad been in a fight, had she been attacked, or were those the scars of war? *She did say she was in the military, didn't she?* Perhaps Chad had gotten caught by one of the roadside bombs or something while serving. The idea someone would inflict those kinds of injuries made Reagan physically ill. She held her stomach and started to dry heave. The anger and power it took to push a knife into someone's body was such a foreign concept. Reagan broke out in a cold sweat thinking about it. She wet a washcloth and dabbed her temples and neck, but it was no use, she was going to be sick. Lifting the lid to the toilet, she wretched each time she thought about the scars littering Chad's body. Her stomach cramped each time she dry heaved. Standing, she took a deep breath and held it for a count of ten. *Think about something else,* she pleaded with herself.

It was time she paid attention to what was going on around her. She had been so oblivious to the group of people around her. Reagan wasn't like that in her business life and wondered why she had taken this attitude with her personal safety. It was time for a change and she knew the only one who could do so was Reagan herself.

"Are you all right?"

Reagan looked at the door and sighed, she would have to put on a professional face and ignore what she'd seen. "I'm good."

"Open the door, Ms. Reynolds."

"Just a minute," Reagan said, dabbing her face and wiping her mouth. Trying to compose herself, she freshened up her make-up, ran her hands down her dress, and took a deep cleansing breath before walking out of the bathroom. "Sorry, I think I'm having some after effects from last night."

Chad reached up and touched her face. "You

look a little pale. Perhaps, we need to go in and have you checked out?"

"I'll be fine. Is that coffee I smell?" She walked past Chad. "Sophia, the coffee smells wonderful. Can I have a cup please?"

Chapter Fourteen

The warmth of the day was setting in early, and the air conditioning was doing little to keep Chad cool. There was no way she could lose the jacket and expose her gun, which meant by lunch time she would have to change into a fresh shirt. Reagan didn't help matters in her office-drag of high heels, short skirt, and sleeveless blouse, tucked neatly into the tight skirt. Clearly, she had changed from her tight dress from earlier—not that Chad noticed. Her long legs delicately crossed at the ankles and angled across the seat kept Chad's attention each time Reagan fidgeted in her seat. She pulled her skirt down and adjusted her position for the tenth time, but who was counting?

Trying to divert her attention, she checked her watch again and noted the time. At this rate they would be early for Reagan's first meeting with Alex Hamilton, the first and longest sitting board member. Chad had done extensive background checks on all the board members and Mr. Hamilton was so clean she wouldn't be surprised if he squeaked when he walked in today. Looking back at Reagan, Chad watched the way she rolled the watch on her wrist, then tapped it with her long nail. If she was nervous, this was the only tick Chad could see. The businesswoman sitting in front of her was a far cry from the child-like woman she found curled up in her arms last night. She woke in the middle of the night to find her nose buried in the soft locks splayed out in front of her. Every time she tried to disengage, Reagan mewed and moaned, moving closer to Chad. She finally stopped moving when Reagan threw a leg over her hip and slid her hand along her ribs.

"Can I ask you a question?" Reagan said, pulling Chad from her tingling memories.

"Depends, is it work related?"

"Sorta." Reagan lightly tapped her watch and then looked up, searching Chad's eyes.

"Sure."

"I...a...well first let me apologize again for barging in this morning."

"I've already forgotten about it."

"Okay. I couldn't help but notice..." Reagan twisted her watch again.

Chad knew what was coming, a question about her scars, but if Reagan thought she was going to spill her guts just because she caught her in an awkward moment, she should think again. This was probably the time to have a talk about boundaries.

"You have a tattoo on your chest. What does it mean?"

Surprised, Chad rolled her eyebrows together and studied Reagan. If she was trying to go in through the back door to get information the way she had with Marcus, she wanted to rethink her plan of attack. Chad reached up and touched her chest where the ink sat. As if the scars weren't reminder enough, she had inked herself, taking back her power, but it also carried a double meaning. She would never allow another woman to control her life as Dawn had.

"It's Latin for, 'never again'," Chad offered.

"Why?"

"Why?"

"Yeah, why, 'never again'?"

Chad shrugged her shoulders. "It's personal."

"I see."

"Is that it?"

"Does it have to do with the scars I saw earlier?"

"I told you its personal."

"I'm sorry for what happened."

Chad's eyebrows bunched as she squinted at Reagan. "You've no idea what happened, so why would you be sorry?"

"You're right. I don't know what happened to you but whatever happened, it was brutal." Reagan bowed her head, dropping her eyes to her hands. "You don't get scars like those by accident." She raised her head and locked eyes with Chad. "Do you?"

Chad tried to swallow the lump caught in her throat. She could handle confrontation, but talking about her scars, that was different. "Ms. Reynolds, my personal life is off limits for discussion. I'm here to protect you and we need to focus on that. So," Chad pulled a pad from the inside pocket, opened it and continued, "I have you meeting Mr. Alex Hamilton. I've done an extensive background check on Mr. Hamilton and he's clean. Following him, I have you down to see Mr. White and—"

"Hold on. How many are you going to schedule in a day? These things take time. I need time to talk to them, discuss upcoming contracts, and where they see the company five, ten or twenty years from now."

"How long do you need to discuss business?"

"I figured I would talk to Uncle Alex, and then we could have lunch and finalize an agreement. That's going to take the better part of the day."

"Really?"

"Yes, really. I didn't know I was on a timeline, Ms. Morgan."

"I assumed you would need an hour or so with each board member to handle your business."

"Obviously you don't know how the corporate world works. In your world you might be able to conclude your business in an hour or less, but in the business world it's all about negotiations and sometimes those can take weeks or months."

"You're not saying this could take months are you? If so, I'll have to rearrange the board members who are traveling in to meet with you and meet them at their locations instead." Chad could feel a pang of urgency shoot through her. Months were not what she had planned when she took on this job, and the thought of working day in and day out for months with Regan was starting to look more like a nightmare and not a dream job. Great, now she had to break it to her team that the job might last longer, much longer.

The car coasted to a stop back at their original hotel. The door swung open as Sophia stuck her head in.

"We're here, Chad."

"Thanks, Sophia, can you give me a minute?"

Turning towards Reagan, she took a deep breath and let out her usual perfunctory sigh.

"Relax, Ms. Morgan. I know the rules." Reagan smoothed her hair back, tucking the loose, unruly strands back into her bun. "I don't plan on ditching you again, so if you don't mind can we get on with this?"

"Of course, Ms. Reynolds." Chad swept her arm towards the open door and followed Reagan out. "Go ahead and park. I'll text you when we're on our way down," Chad whispered to Sophia.

"You got it."

Holding the hotel door open, the swaying hips in front of her gave her a brief excuse to smile. Nodding to the front desk, she punched the elevator button for the penthouse. Their meeting would take place in a conference room on the same floor close to Reagan's original suite. Chad watched for any signs of anxiety as the elevator climbed closer to the penthouse. If Reagan was nervous, she was hiding it well. Chad would expect anyone in Reagan's position had a right to be scared, even panic, but not Reagan. The way she stood, her back straight, the tight dress accentuating her strong shoulders and full hips made Chad wonder what was under all that pride. Was she someone who melted when she was back in her room or did she carry it all inside and eventually have a colossal meltdown at a later point? She was stoic, calm, and rigid as she watched the floors click by on the panel.

"Are you cruising me, Ms. Morgan?" Reagan said, eyeing Chad's reflection in the polished brass button panel.

"Excuse me?"

"Were you checking out my ass, Ms. Morgan?"

"No, of course not."

"Ms. Morgan, I know you think I'm a simpleton, but let me assure you I know when someone is checking me out." Reagan shifted her briefcase to her other had and turned towards Chad. "For example, you were checking me out in my home, and then again in my father's office, and as for your staff, I could count on two hands how many times they've checked me out."

Chad sighed and shook her head at Reagan's

arrogance. It figured she would imagine everyone in the room would be trying to get into her pants. Did most high-powered business types think their life of privilege entitled them to sleep with whomever they wanted, even the help?

"You don't believe me, do you? You think I imagine everyone wants to get into my pants, don't you?"

"Well the thought had crossed my mind, yes," Chad said, feeling as if Reagan had read her mind in her accurate assessment of the woman.

"Hmm, okay how much are you willing to bet?"

"Bet?"

"Yes, put your money where you mouth is. I bet I can tell you exactly what's going to happen when we meet with Alex Hamilton."

"That's because you know him."

"No, it's because I know men."

Chad took in Reagan's appearance, from her high heels, to her perfectly coiffed hair. There was no doubt she was easy on the eyes, but her assumption every guy wanted to fuck her was beyond an over-inflated ego.

"Look, any woman who doesn't admit she uses her sexuality to get what she wants is lying." Reagan's eyebrows peaked as Chad rolled her eyes at the statement. "Okay, any woman, but you. You, I would put on the side of men," Chad said, chiding Reagan in her observation.

"You think I want to get into your pants? Geez."

Chad crossed her arms at the statement and frowned. She had been compared to many things but a sex-starved member of the male species was rarely one of them.

"Look, if I'm full of crap, you win."

"What do I get if I win?" Suddenly, Chad was intrigued with the possibility of winning. She was just competitive enough to take Reagan up on the challenge and if it taught the ego driven businesswoman a lesson, she was doubly benefited.

Reagan tapped her hips with her index finger, looking as if she was lost in thought. "What do you want?"

"Shorter meetings."

"That's it? You don't want to wager a little bet?"

"Nope, I want to finish all of this and get you home safe and sound."

"Okay," Reagan said, smiling.

"What do you want?" Chad said, waiting for some outlandish request.

"Dinner and you tell me how you got those scars."

"Nope."

"If you're so confident I'm full of shit, what's the problem?"

What was the problem indeed? Chad read people like most women read romance novels, and if she was half right about men, Reagan would be closer to being right than she would be. She could judge a book by its cover, but she had to see the book first and she only knew the board members from what she had read. All were happily married men with much to lose if they strayed. Then again, men in power were a different breed.

"Dinner? Why dinner?"

"I'm sick of being cooped up. I was supposed to be on vacation, but all I've done is see the inside of my room or a car and I'm sick of it."

"Aren't you being a little dramatic?"

"No, aren't you being a little paranoid?"

"I'm paid to be paranoid."

"Okay just dinner."

"I can do dinner," Chad said, pulling her cell phone out. She would call her team and get them to make the arrangements and recon a restaurant. Before she could start texting, Reagan grabbed her hand.

"No team and I get to pick the restaurant."

"No."

"What, you can't handle my protection personally?"

"Of course, but—"

"No, take it or leave it."

"Seriously?"

"Look we're going to get out of this elevator. Uncle Alex is going to give me a hug a very long hug. Then he's going to rub me across his chest by rocking me in a hug, to disguise his lecherous behavior. Then he'll grasp my hand in both of his, compliment me on how I've changed since the last time he's seen me. When he shakes my hand his eyes will look at my breasts, then he'll smile again. He'll pull me in close, tucking me under his arm as he wraps his arm around my shoulders, and walk me to the conference room. All the while he'll run his hand up and down my back, where his hand will finally rest on the top of my ass as he escorts me to the couch."

Chad felt her temper rise as Reagan described the abhorrent behavior she knew was coming. If she knew all of this, how could she put herself in the position to be viewed as a sexual object and not taken seriously as the business woman she was? Behavior like that was not only disgusting, it was sexist.

"How can you let someone treat you like that,

especially if you know its coming? All the more reason to have someone with you when you meet these bastards," Chad confessed angrily.

"Because I have to."

"No one has to knowingly subject themselves to that type of behavior."

"I'm taking over one of the largest military sub-contracting companies. I'm the only woman in a CEO position. If you think I'm going to let a little groping push me off track, you better think again." Reagan glared at Chad. "I've worked hard to get here. I'm not going down without a fight."

"After what happened last night, Ms. Reynolds, I'm surprised you're still willing to put yourself through all of this."

"First, can you just call me Reagan? I'm getting a little tired of hearing *Ms. Reynolds* this and *Ms. Reynolds* that." Reagan cocked her head waiting for a reply to her request.

"Of course, Ms. Reynolds. I mean Reagan."

"Good, now for your observation. I need to be strong for my father, the company, and all the employees who work for us. They're counting on the company for their livelihood. So, I don't have time to freak-out. Besides, what's done is done. Right?"

"I applaud your positive take on the situation."

"I guess I didn't check the option box when I decided to do this," Reagan said, smoothing down her dress.

Both women looked up when the elevator dinged, signaling their arrival at the penthouse floor. Chad stepped out first and looked down the hallway before motioning Reagan to exit.

"Besides," Reagan said as she took Chad's arm.

"Why should I be afraid? I have you to protect me, don't I?"

"Of course." Chad patted her hand, suddenly feeling uncomfortable with Reagan's arm wrapped around hers.

"Reggie, I thought I heard the elevator."

A tall, grey-haired gentleman came out of the conference room with his arms wide.

"Uncle Alex! How are you? I've missed you. You didn't come for the holidays this year."

"I'm sorry. The kids wanted to go skiing, so we went to Aspen. How is your father?"

Reagan kissed her uncle on both cheeks and then threaded her arm through his as they walked to the conference room. If Chad didn't know better she would have actually thought Alex was her real uncle, but watching the two together gave Chad a funny feeling. Suddenly, she wanted to stand between the two and push Alex away from Reagan. The familiarity he used to touch her, to talk to her, aggravated Chad. In fact, the urge to protect Reagan took control of her thoughts as the two sat together on the couch. The way Reagan threw her head back and laughed at the stupid jokes floating in the room heightened Chad's need to get between them.

Chad felt as if she wasn't even in the room as the conversation drifted around, touching on family, schools and vacations. She couldn't relate to skiing in Aspen, snorkeling in Bermuda, or even taking a month off to travel Europe. The world these two lived in was visibly different than the one Chad survived in. As she studied Reagan from her position across the room, she noticed a nervous tick as Reagan stroked her crossed legs at the calf. She had done the same thing to Chad when she was in the corporate offices. Looking up, she locked eyes with Reagan, who smiled briefly and shook her head. Once again she had been caught.

Clearing her throat, she stood and walked towards Reagan and Alex.

"If you'll excuse me for a moment," Chad said, looking at Reagan then Alex. "I need to check in."

"Of course, Chad."

As she walked away, she heard Alex question Reagan. "You didn't introduce us Reggie? Who is she?"

This should be interesting, thought Chad, slowing down to hear the response.

"Oh, Chad is a friend from college and is my traveling companion. I know its old fashioned, but Dad insisted I bring someone with me. When we're done we're going to take a short vacation."

"Is this someone special, Reggie?"

"What? Oh, no, no she's just a good friend, Uncle."

"Well, she doesn't say much does she?"

"She's a little shy. I told her she could stay in the room, but she wanted to see how the business world functions."

"I see, well since we're talking about business, how are things at the company?"

"I glad you asked," Reagan said, putting her briefcase on the coffee table.

Chad smiled at the lame excuse she gave her uncle. Clearly, she wasn't good at lying.

Chapter Fifteen

Reagan closed her eyes and let her head rest on the back of the couch. The last hour had been brutal. Between fending off Alex's lame advances and his rapid-fire suggestions about the changes Reynolds Holdings should make to position itself for the future, Reagan's head was ready to explode. She had watched Chad come in and out of the meeting, each time making brief eye contact with her and motioning to her watch as if Reagan could shut the man up. Each time she had guided the conversation to his support of her taking over as CEO, Alex had mumbled something about proper successors and bloodlines. Whatever the hell that meant. By the end she had almost told him to screw off, but instead reminded herself she needed his support. Hell, she almost wished she had let him touch her just so she had something to hold over his head.

She slipped off her heels and wiggled her toes, hoping to stave off the charley horse she knew was coming from wearing the high heels too long. Her body ached from sitting so straight, with her legs elegantly tucked to the side and crossed at the ankles. Unfortunately, she realized in her youth her power wasn't in her intellect, but her body. A female college professor had pulled her aside one day and said as much.

"Reagan, women who are beautiful have an advantage over our male counterparts. Your beauty will

get you in the door. It's what you do once you're in the door that's important. You have to be twice as smart as the guys. You'll always need to be one step ahead of them. Don't be afraid to turn the tables."

Whether it was sage advice or not, Reagan observed how girls at college would twist a professor or two around their little finger. Most of the time they weren't the most attractive, but they were cunning. There should have been a class in Men-101, because being smart didn't seem to matter as much as being sexy did. The idea of using her sexuality to get what she wanted didn't sit well with her at first, but after seeing how it was done, she didn't regret using the one tool she could control—herself. It wasn't her fault if men thought they were getting something else when they weren't. They had set the rules, not her, and if she had to out think them then they deserved what little respect she had for them. The only man who had treated her with any respect was her father and she never resorted to playing games with him.

"Ready?" A low voice whispered.

Reagan responded without opening her eyes. "If you only knew." Sitting up, she rubbed her neck and reached for the hand Chad extended. "So did you like the show?"

"I hate to say you're right, but you're right. He's a dog."

"Yes, well one dog down and a whole pack to go."

"Are they all going to be like that?"

"Not all, but enough. So, I get to choose where we're having dinner, then?"

"Sure."

Reagan was surprised at how relaxed Chad

was after a long day of waiting. If the roles had been reversed, she knew after an hour she would be walking the hallway like a neurotic dog pacing its kennel.

"Seriously?"

"Seriously. After what I witnessed, you're lucky I didn't come in there and rip his head off. The bastard."

"Oh, Alex is harmless, especially after I reminded him his daughter is the same age as I am. Seemed to put things in perspective for a moment." Reagan smiled, knowing she had practically accused him of being a child molester by reminding him that taking him up on his advances would be comparable to sleeping with his daughter. The conversation had been all business after that, with Alex assuring her of his support. Reagan thanked him on her father's behalf and allowed him to leave with a modicum of his dignity intact.

"I don't know how you do it, Reagan." Chad reached for Reagan's briefcase and jacket.

"The playing field isn't level for women, Ms. Morgan."

"Chad."

"Chad. We have to use every tool available to us, and even then the game is still tilted against us."

"Well, I guess it's why I do what I do. At least I get to shoot the bad guys. You have to humor them, coddle them, and hope they vote your way."

"Oh, they will, trust me. When I'm finished with them they'll not only vote my way, they'll be praying I don't sue them for sexual harassment."

"I'm sure."

Reagan leaned against the elevator wall and sighed. If the rest of the board members were anything like Alex, she had her work cut out for her. The small elevator suddenly closed in on Reagan as she dropped her shoes and keeled over, hitting the floor shoulder first.

"Reagan!"

Trying to focus, Reagan's head swam as she watched the roof of the elevator blur and then sharpen, then blur again. She could feel Chad's warm hand touch her face as she turned and tried to look at her, but couldn't see her. She tried to talk, but her mouth felt like it was full of cotton.

"Don't move. I think you hit your head when you fainted."

Fainted, she hadn't fainted, had she? Grasping Chad's arm, she tried to right herself into a sitting position, but Chad held her down.

"Don't move."

"I'm fine, stop. Let me up. I just need to get the hell out of this elevator. It's too hot in here. Please—"

Without warning, she was swooped up into Chad's arms and held tightly against the woman's chest. The smell of soap and lemons engulfed her and she felt light-headed again. Grateful for the comfort and safety, she leaned her head against Chad's strong chest and relaxed. The elevator dinged when it hit the lobby floor and without hesitation, Chad bolted for the door of the hotel.

"What happened?" Reagan heard Sophia ask as she stood holding the limo door open.

"She fainted in the elevator."

"Is she all right?"

"I don't know, we need to get her to the hospital."

"No!" Reagan struggled to get out of Chad's arms. "I'm not going. Put me down."

Chad set Reagan gently on the seat of the open limo and kneeled down in front of her.

"You fainted. People just don't faint without a reason."

"I'm fine. I...the elevator...I mean, I just panicked. It happened so fast, I just...." Reagan rubbed the pain in her shoulder and winced.

"We should at least get that shoulder checked out," Chad suggested.

"No, I'm fine. I haven't eaten all day and I'm probably still a little woozy from last night. Can we just get something to eat, please?" Reagan pleaded. "I'm sure I'll be fine afterwards. If not, you have my permission to take me in for medical treatment."

Chad cupped Reagan's chin and gazed into her eyes. She wrenched her chin away from Chad's prying view and slid across the seat, leaning her head against it. She was more embarrassed than hurt, but admitting this to Chad was not going to happen. Chad had already seen her at her weakest and that would never happen again.

"Any word on the flower delivery yet?" Chad asked Sophia.

"Not yet. Marcus thinks he has a lead, but he needs to check one more thing."

"Okay, call the team and tell them we're getting some dinner and they should do the same."

"You got it."

"Oh, and Sophia, make sure they know we're cutting the trip in half."

Reagan tried to sit up but the world started spinning again, so she sat back before Chad could see her sway. If Chad thought she was calling the shots, she had another thing coming. The sound of the car door shutting made her open her eyes. Before she could say anything Chad was speaking.

"Relax, I know what you're going to say, but I have to think about your safety if you won't. I suggest we finish up the few appointments you have here and reschedule the rest."

"You don't get it, do you?"

"No, I do get it, but if you pass out during a meeting, who looks weak and inept then? Huh?"

Reagan shook her head and sat silently looking out the window. Her feet ached, her head was still swimming, and her ego was a little more than bruised. Chad was right, if she had fainted in front of Alex or another board member she'd have some explaining to do. Her health would be an excuse for the board to eliminate her from inheriting control of the company.

"How's your head?"

"Fine, not as bruised as my ego."

"Why? You only fainted Reagan, you weren't drunk and dancing on a table in some bar."

"Funny." She half-heartedly smiled at Chad.

"Perspective, Reagan. Keep it all in perspective."

Reagan kept her eyes closed as she flexed her feet and winced. The heels would be the first things to go when she made CEO. Well, maybe not completely, her shoe fetish would just have to become accustomed to a wedge or a nice set of flats every once in a while.

"Here, give me your feet."

"What?"

Chad patted her lap and motioned for Reagan's feet. "Let me see your feet. I'm sure they must be killing you wearing those damn things." Chad pointed to Reagan's footwear.

Without protest, Reagan rested her feet on Chad's

lap and sighed when she felt the firm pressure of Chad's thumb knead her heel. Reagan smiled embarrassingly as the instant gratification of the massage escaped her lips in the form of a moan.

"Any chance we could get that masseuse back? I would trade dinner for a massage."

"You need to eat more than you need a massage, so the answer is no, but I might be persuaded to call her back tomorrow. One condition," Chad said as she continued to press against the sole of Reagan's foot.

"Anything."

"You cut the trip in half until we find out who's behind the death threats."

Silence lingered between the two as one considered her options and the other focused on the foot massage she was giving, knowing this would be a one-sided negotiation. Gripping Reagan's foot, she continued to push against the heel that suddenly seemed to be resisting against her thumbs. Tweaking an eyebrow in Reagan's direction, Chad smiled and slightly nodded her head. "You now know how dangerous this situation can be. I need a little more time to set a trap for whoever is getting access to your information. I think we need to go underground, so to speak, for a week at the most."

"Take me to dinner and let's talk about it."

"Mexican okay?"

"Sounds delicious."

Keying the intercom, Chad instructed, "Sophia, let's go to that Mexican restaurant I sent you directions for earlier."

"Yes, ma'am."

"You were going to take me to dinner the whole time weren't you?"

Chad flashed a quick smile and then briefly gave a nod. "After watching board members in action, I figured you were right. I realized this is your world and I'm just a visitor. I need to step back and let you do your job and I need to step forward and do mine. Hence, the recommendation to go into hiding until I can smoke out the rat in your organization."

"You really think it's someone inside the company?"

"How else did they find out what hotel you were in? I only changed it after you dumped me at the airport. You, the team, and your father were the only ones who knew."

"This sucks. Everyone's been with the company for years. I can't think of any new hires or anyone who's been fired recently who would go to this length to get back at Reynolds."

"I don't have the answers yet, but I will. Don't worry, at least I know you're safe."

Reagan settled deeper into the leather seat and tried to relax. "Well, I'm definitely in your hands," Reagan said, indicating her feet nestled in Chad's lap. "Literally."

Chad smiled. "Yep." She squeezed Reagan's foot. "Literally."

Chapter Sixteen

L ittle drops of water slid down the sweating margarita glass. The salt was practically gone and yet the glass was only half empty. Reagan had watched Chad lick the coarse pieces, tongue them against the roof of her mouth and then sip the drink, gently smacking her lips at the sour taste. She hadn't seen someone take so much pleasure in a drink in a long time and it made her smile.

"What's the smile for?"

"Hmm?"

"What's the smile for?"

Reagan dipped a chip in salsa, shoved it in her mouth, and then pointed at her lips as if saying she couldn't talk. She slowly worked the chip over before taking a sip from her wine to wash it down. The conversation had been lacking ever since they had sat down, but the alcohol seemed to be loosening lips, so to speak, and Reagan wanted to approach the subject of Chad's scars carefully. Like a dog with a bone, she wasn't about to let Chad off so easily.

"So what did you think about today's meeting?"

"Me?" Chad said, touching her fingertips to her chest. "You're asking me?"

"Sure. Why not?"

"Reagan, I'm not a business person, so my opinion doesn't matter."

"But you study people. You assess a situation

and make a decision or do something based on another person actions. I'm interested in your assessment," Reagan said, wiping some lipstick from her wine glass. "I don't usually have the opportunity to ask someone what they think of something. I'm usually the one who makes the decisions based on my own assessment."

"Okay, since you asked, I think Alex Hamilton is an ass," Chad threw out. "If the rest of the board members are going to act like this, I'm going to have a difficult time sitting idly by and watching them paw at you."

"Interesting," Reagan said demurely.

"You asked."

"Yes I did, I'm just surprised at your response."

"Why? Do you think I'm indifferent to your situation?"

"I just didn't expect you to be so..." Reagan studied Chad for a moment. "Possessive."

Reagan locked eyes with Chad almost challenging her to deny the accusation. Instead, Chad's look of longing surprised her. Her heart jumped a beat as she followed Chad's finger tracing an imaginary path over the tablecloth, almost touching her own outstretched hand. She pulled it back for fear she might combust at the thought of Chad touching her. She quirked an eyebrow and grabbed her wine glass to mask her reaction. Why she was suddenly worried Chad might touch her? Chad had been professional, efficient, and charitable, even as she pushed the woman to her limits only days earlier. Running her tongue over her lips, she shivered thinking about Chad's muscular body earlier. Feeling like a teenager in lust, she had lain next to the woman all night, childishly wishing Chad would accidentally touch her. Chad's hand stroking down her arm had kept her awake half the night, but more importantly, it had stoked a burning she hadn't felt in a while. The security of an innocent embrace tormented her sleep. Perhaps it was the kind of attraction one had for someone who saved her life? Or perhaps the take-charge attitude Chad displayed while ordering everyone around as she waited for the ambulance had twisted her reality about the woman. Closing her eyes, she floated back to the only dream of the night she could remember.

A hand splayed across her stomach, gently kneading the soft skin beneath its touch. She felt it move along her ribs, then stop when it barely touched her breast. Her mind willed it to go further, yet Chad's hand rested a moment longer before her thumb caressed the soft side and then touched the underside of her breast. A surge shot through her body as Chad cupped it and smoothed her hand back and forth underneath the soft, pliant skin.

Pinch my nipple, she begged in her mind.

Leaning back against Chad, she opened herself, her legs parting, inviting Chad's touch. The invitation was accepted and her skin burned from the path of warmth left behind as Chad's hand skimmed the length of her body to her pussy. She jumped slightly when she felt Chad's lips gently pull on her neck at the same time her fingers slid between her outer lips, opening her further. The tip of a finger swirled around in the entrance before—"

"Reagan." Chad's voice smashed the dream and startled Reagan. "Sorry, I didn't mean to wake you. Maybe we should just get the food to go and get you home so you can sleep."

Blushing, Reagan took a quick sip of her wine,

trying to push the memory from her mind. The warmth of the restaurant was affecting her, or maybe it was dreaming of Chad practically ready to take control over her body. She more accurately thought it was probably the alcohol. Struggling to peel off her jacket, Chad slid around the booth and pulled on the sleeve as she wrestled with it. Her skin prickled where Chad's hand touched her arm just as it had in her dream as she pulled her elbow free of the twisted sleeve.

"Thank you."

"No problem."

"I'm sorry I wasn't sleeping...I...I was just thinking about something," she said, finishing her wine. Fanning her face, she couldn't shake the blush that seemed to be a permanent state now. "Isn't it hot in here to you?"

"No, it's rather nice. Maybe you're still feeling the effects of the drugs?"

"Hmm."

"Maybe I should tell the waiter to box our order up?"

"No, I don't want to go back to the house yet. I don't think I could handle being cooped up right now. Besides, it's nice to be away from everything, to forget for at least a little while."

Reagan stretched like a cat sitting on a warm windowsill. Her dress pulled tightly across her body. She watched Chad's gaze dart from her breasts, to her face, and then across the room. A blush was Reagan's reward for the innocent enough action. It was clear she wasn't the only one touched with a bit of lust, if Chad's reaction reflected her thoughts.

The waiter returned, flirting with Reagan as he refilled her glass. She caught him saying something about the heat of the food matching the heat of the room, all the while she stared at Chad. Another slow burn worked its way through her body as Chad undid another button on her shirt. As her jacket opened a bit, Reagan could see dark metal barely peeking out from underneath. If she were honest with herself, she had to admit she was turned on thinking about Chad harnessing all that raw power. Dominating it with her strong, adept hands and bringing it all under her control.

Reagan slid her fingers along the stem of her wine glass and felt her body tingle as she imagined surrendering to those strong hands. Her body ached for relief, but wouldn't come until she got back to her room and her toy bag. Reagan's tongue slipped out and ran along her lips, wetting them. Chad's eyes followed its path, biting her own lip as she blushed again. A blushing Chad was an interesting thought to Reagan. In fact, she had briefly toyed with the idea of flirting with the dark, brooding woman, but let it go when things had taken a turn for the worse after the airport fiasco. The sight of the scars didn't detract from Chad's stark good looks. They only added to the mystery of the woman seated across from her, stroking her wet margarita glass.

"Another Margarita for my friend, please," Reagan said, ignoring Chad's denial. "I'm the boss remember? Besides it's the least I can do since you had to sit through hours of boring meetings."

"I don't usually drink while I'm on a job."

"Well, I appreciate you making an exception this one time. Besides, I don't like to drink alone." Another sip from her glass kept her from locking eyes with Chad and kept her mouth busy.

"Maybe you should put your," Reagan nodded in the direction of Chad's weapon, "thing in the car and take your jacket off and relax. You seem a little tense."

"Ms. Reynolds—"

"Reagan."

"Reagan, I'm on the job and I don't take my gun off, especially not after what happened last night." Chad stirred the ice cubes of her margarita, clinking them against the glass.

"Do I make you nervous?"

"What?"

"Well, you seem to be off your game ever since this morning. When I..." Reagan gestured the length of her own body, trying to delicately indicate the scars which littered Chad's.

"I'm not off my game and if you think you're getting short-changed in my ability to protect you just because you saw my scars, I'm more than happy to call Marcus and let him shadow you for the remainder of the meetings." Chad's look was dismissive as she motioned to the waiter.

Reagan reached across the table, grabbing Chad's hand and forcing it back down. "Look, I didn't mean anything, I mean I wasn't implying, well you know...I mean, well you just seemed...embarrassed. I mean... oh hell, I don't know what I mean." Reagan closed her eyes and sighed. Being at a loss for words wasn't her style, but the jolt of energy that sped through her body from the contact with Chad's hand was offsetting. The thoughtless caress across Chad's knuckles infused her body with warmth, and had Chad giving her a smirk. Hardly the touch of a boss and employee. Reagan dropped the hand as if it were a burning ember.

"I'm sorry, I don't know what's come over me."

Before Chad could respond, instructions not to touch the hot plates of food interrupted the exchange. Both women focused on their own thoughts and food.

Chapter Seventeen

Chad had barely tasted the food as she measured each bite, chewed, and swallowed. It wasn't that she didn't like Mexican food. No, her dinner companion made the food bland. The not-so-innocent touch, the endless innuendos, and the sudden urge to lay waste to Reagan's lips had her spun tightly. It had taken every bit of willpower last night not to touch Reagan as she lay against Chad. The way Reagan's tight ass had fit neatly against Chad, reminded her of the first night she had met Reagan at her home. That lead to the memory of the naked breast that had accidently been exposed, which now lead to her sudden discomfort. A nice neat little package had literally been in her lap, and now sat directly across from her, blatantly flirting with her.

Chad slid her tongue across the new rim of salt and gently licked at it. The cool lime taste of the drink was followed by the warm caress through her body, ending at her center. If alcohol was supposed to relax someone, it was having the opposite effect on Chad. It enhanced the burning desire she felt starting to form in the pit of her stomach.

"Oh God, I guess I'm hungrier than I thought." Reagan's look was sultry. At least that's how it felt to the over stimulated Chad. "I guess practically falling on your face can work up an appetite. Aren't you hungry?"

Chad pushed her food around on her plate and forced a forkful down before answering. "Oh, um yeah, I—"

Reagan reached over with her fork, speared a piece of grilled chicken from Chad's plate, and popped it in her mouth.

"Oh," Reagan closed her eyes. "This is good." The emphasis on *good* trailed into a low moan.

A jolt speared at Chad's nipples, sliding down her spine, and depositing itself between her legs. In any other situation, Chad would have gotten up and walked out without looking back, but Reagan was her charge and she couldn't very well leave her. *Could she? No, of course she couldn't.* She chastised herself for even considering the thought. *Handle your business, Chad.* She mentally shook herself and took another drink of her margarita.

"Water, please," she said motioning to the waiter.

"Are you okay?"

"Reagan, I think we should get going. I have a lot of work that still needs to be done back at the house. You have to get ready for your meetings tomorrow." Chad wiped her mouth and tossed her napkin on her plate. Reagan had a slight slur to her words, nothing anyone else would have noticed, but Chad was paid to be observant and she had seen the bottle empty quicker than she would have liked.

"I'm sorry I made you nervous, Chad."

Reagan's impish grin made Chad question the sincerity of her statement.

"I assure you I'm not nervous, Ms. Reynolds," Chad said, hoping the formality of her response would clue Reagan in she was reestablishing professional boundaries.

"Afraid you'll admit something you know we're both feeling?"

"Ms. Reynolds, I think you assume too much. A few glasses of wine, or a margarita or two doesn't change the fact that while I might find you attractive, my job is to protect you, not to fuck you."

Both women raised their eyes at the proclamation.

"Ms. Morgan, I am more than a little aware of the power dynamic here," Reagan said, before dabbing her napkin at the corners of her mouth. I'm your employer and yet I find myself under your control. You are my protector, so to speak, and as such we must walk a fine line between those two positions. Correct?"

"Obviously."

"Good. Then as two professionals, we can have an adult conversation, wouldn't you agree?"

Chad knew Reagan was baiting her, but played along anyway. "I'd like to think so."

"Good, now I know you're attracted to me and clearly I'm attracted to you," Reagan stated, putting up her hand to stop the protest she knew was coming from Chad.

Chad wondered on what planet Reagan would think she had given Chad any signs of interest. She had dumped Chad at the airport, planting baby powder and a knife in the hopes of ditching her protection. Then she had said and done things any woman in her right mind would have called cruel and downright nasty. It was clear Reagan lived in her own world, with her own set of rules to run that world. Yes, Chad had to admit she had indulged in innocent touches when she massaged Reagan, and yes, she had wondered what it would be like to slide her hand under Reagan's shirt as she laid tucked up against her last night, but she never telegraphed her intentions in any way.

"I saw it in your eyes that first night in my home. I'm sure you remember, you had my arm behind my back and your front pressed against my ass." Reagan held her hand up again in an attempt to stop any denials from Chad and continued, "From the way you looked at me when my robe opened, I'd have to say I've seen starving men look more disinterested in a meal than how your eyes devoured me. I would have sworn you were about to eat me up that night, Ms. Morgan. Am I right?"

Chad flinched at the assessment. She wasn't about to confirm Reagan's suspicions so easily, besides if she confirmed what Reagan said, it would only inflate her already oversized, self-absorbed opinion of herself. Chad didn't need any more problems with a woman who thought so highly of herself.

"Well, you are the expert at people watching, as you say."

"So you aren't denying you find me attractive?"

"Ms. Reynolds, I really don't think this is appropriate conversation, do you?"

"Don't dodge the question, Ms. Morgan. I know you find me attractive and I shall confirm your suspicions. I am a lesbian and I find you—"

"Ms. Reynolds, stop before you say something you'll regret when you're a bit more sober than you are now."

"Oh trust me, I'm sober and I know exactly what I'm saying."

"Okay, so I'll play if it will get us out of here without you making a scene. What is it you find about me to your liking?"

"Well you have a—butch swagger about you that is damn captivating." Reagan smiled at the revelation.

"Really?"

"Hmm, really." Reagan paused, looking like she was searching for the perfect word, or she was just a little too drunk and it was affecting her ability to function. "You're not my usual type, actually."

"Ah, good to know. What is your usual type, Ms. Reynolds?"

Chad could almost guess the answer without even trying. Women like Reagan were high maintenance. They required all of their lover's attention and often withheld their own while they ran their lovers ragged. At least it had been her experience with women who thought wine qualified as a food group and caviar was a vegetable when served on sour cream and a cracker. No, Chad had Reagan pegged to the wall and didn't need to hear how femme women dated other femme women who rotated Gucci bags as often as they changed their silk dainties.

"Honestly, I find confidence a huge turn-on. In the business world you rarely meet confident, successful women who don't want something from you."

Chad almost felt sorry for her own warped perspective of women. Reagan lived in a world where everyone wanted something from her. Her money, her company, her body—but not her, not the woman underneath all of those things that came wrapped in a tight little package she flaunted under Chad's nose. Chad watched as Reagan ran a finger across her lips contemplatively. Something bit at Reagan's self-reflection and Chad couldn't put her finger on it, yet.

"There's the *executive bunny lounge*, as I like to

call it."

Chad quirked her head at the statement, not sure what to make of the *executive bunny lounge*. She had never heard of such a place, but if it was anything like the Bunny Ranch in Nevada, maybe she needed to make a pit stop after this job.

"Oh you know the place, it's the bar or lounge where all the executives go to relax, have a drink, and talk shop. If you were to ask all the office assistants at work where that place was, they could tell you and they could tell you which executives hang-out there."

"Really?"

"Yes, really. If you don't believe me, ask Marcy, my father's assistant. It's how we met and started dating."

"Wait. You're dating Marcy, your father's executive assistant?"

Shit, how could Chad have not known such an important fact about Reagan? She needed a moment to digest the information. It hadn't shown up on any background check, or in any interview with Marcy's co-workers.

"Not anymore, it wasn't a big deal. We dated gosh, four years ago, maybe five. We were off and on for about three months. Nothing serious, trust me, she wasn't a lesbian. No one knew, we were very discreet. Not even my own father knew." Reagan took another sip of her wine. "It was fun for a while, but we both knew it wouldn't last."

Chad wasn't shocked by Reagan's cavalier attitude about the relationship. In fact, it fit the impression she had of Reagan to a T.

"So that's it? No harm, no foul? It's all good and seeing her everyday doesn't bother either of you?"

"We're both professionals, Chad." Reagan

brushed off Chad's comments as if they were crumbs on the table. "Besides, she moved on rather quickly. She got a promotion as my father's assistant, got a new boyfriend, and got pregnant. I'd say it's a win-win for everyone.

"Interesting."

"What?" Reagan quizzed defensively.

"Nothing. It's why I keep my ex's in the x-files, so I don't have to know what they're doing when it's over."

"Well, to each her own. So where were we? Ah yes, who's my type?"

Chad waited and watched as a slow, deliberate smile worked its way across Reagan's face. She was sure she was in for a seduction at the hands of a professional. Reagan's gaze lingered on Chad's lips and then she flicked her tongue out and let it trail along the bow of her upper lip, darting back in only to be followed by a slow, sensual smile. If trouble had a face, Chad was looking at it right now, in the smoldering blue eyes of a seductress. Yep! She was being played, hard. She was tempted to call a personal foul, but the game had barely started.

"Am I supposed to guess or are you going to tell me? Or perhaps you'd like me to flirt it out of you?"

Now the smile reached Reagan's eyes as she stared at Chad. Demure? No, that wasn't the word to describe Reagan Reynolds right now. Captivating. Nope. Lustful was the term Chad searched for from the first time she had met Reagan. It rolled off her in buckets, each wave pelting the unassuming victim as she tried to enamor them with her sexuality. The problem was, in Chad's mind, Reagan hadn't found one person with whom she connected and could temper all that fire, that heat, which if touched incorrectly, would burn out its unsuspecting victim. Chad surmised Reagan went through lovers because they couldn't match her passion, her intensity, and so they were destined for the stray's category. Those women picked up on a night out, but were promptly cut loose after the night was over. She could be wrong, but it was unlikely.

"Well there's an interesting topic, flirting. Do you flirt, Ms. Morgan?" Reagan seemed to have a silly grin permanently plastered to her face. "No I don't suppose you do, do you?"

"Ms. Reynolds."

"Relax, so you want to know my type," Reagan said, and then looked around the room. "See that woman over there?" She pointed in the direction of a petite brunette, laughing and leaning against a rather large man. "She looks like she could be fun."

"You like a challenge, don't you? Clearly, she's straight and taken."

"Well you know what they say, two drinks away..."

"Hmm."

"I have a thing for brunettes," Reagan whispered. "Like you."

Chad sat in stunned silence for a moment waiting for the laugh that usually followed a joke, but it didn't come.

"Me? What is it about me you think is your type, Ms. Reynolds?"

"Didn't I already explain this to you? I like strong, independent, and charming women."

"I assure you, I'm not charming, Ms. Reynolds."

"Oh, I bet you could charm the pants off me right now if you wanted to, Chad. In fact, I doubt you lack for female company when you want it, do you?"

"Ms. Reynolds, my personal life is off-limits."

"Oh, I know, but we aren't talking about your personal life right now. We're talking about the kind of women I'm attracted to, right?"

Chad shook her head. She wasn't sure what they were talking about anymore. She had lost track somewhere back in the conversation when they started talking about bunnies and brunettes.

"Why don't we drop all of this and just be honest with each other? If you didn't work for me and we had met, say at a party, we would probably be exchanging phone numbers right about now. Right?"

The confident look Reagan gave Chad made her desperate to disagree, but she couldn't. She had already established Reagan was her type. Lying now would only make her look the fool, so she would do what she did best, divert her attention.

Patting her chest, she reached in and pulled her phone as if it had gone off.

"I need to take this." Chad flipped the phone open and looked at Reagan imploringly. "If you'll give me just a minute."

"Of course, I'll just go powder my nose."

A soft push was all it would take right now for Chad to bolt like a scared rabbit. Reagan had come on stronger than a used car salesman. It was obvious when she wanted something she didn't back down. Even being told point blank didn't work. Before Chad could regroup, she spotted Reagan exit the ladies room, smiling seductively in her direction.

"Fuck me," was all Chad could say as she stood.

Chapter Eighteen

The limo was sweltering inside. At least that's how it felt to Reagan. Her dress clung to her like a second skin, making her wish she could peel it off. She wondered if Chad would mind if she disrobed and got comfortable. She had remembered to wear underwear and it even matched. Reagan knew she had come on strong with Chad, but when she wanted something, she wasn't afraid to go after it.

"Aren't you hot in the blazer, Ms. Morgan?"

"I'm fine."

"Why don't you take it off? No one will see you and your big gun doesn't scare me."

"I'm sure it would take a lot more than my big gun to scare you, Ms. Reynolds."

Ignoring the comment, Reagan continued the banter. "By the way, how big is your gun?"

"Which one?"

"Oh, you carry more than one?"

Chad just stared at Reagan. "Ah, trade secret. I see, well you have nothing to fear from me, Ms. Morgan. May I see one of them?"

"Nope."

"Why?"

"They're the tools of my trade, Ms. Reynolds. I'm sure you don't go walking around handing your cell phone to people when they ask to see it."

"Actually, I do," Reagan corrected. "Couldn't

you just take all the bullets out and let me touch it? I've never held one, let alone shot one. Besides, if anything happens to you don't you think I should be able to defend myself?"

"Sophia would take over if anything happened to me, and then if Marcus was around he would have the honor of defending you."

"I see, well since you aren't going to let me touch it can you at least show it to me? What if I promise not to touch it?"

"Fine."

Reagan bolted across the space between them and practically landed in Chad's lap. She was honest when she said she had never held a weapon of any kind before. Now the adrenaline of holding all the power in her hands made her giddy, which surprised her since things rarely excited her anymore. Chad pulled her gun from under her armpit, dropped the clip out, and pulled the slide back, ejecting the bullet and locking the slide in the open position.

"This, Ms. Reynolds, is a typical .380. It's smaller than most because I wear it for concealment. It fits into my shoulder holster and stays well hidden."

"How many bullets does it hold?"

"I have an illegal magazine for this weapon, which holds twelve bullets," Chad stated matter-of-factly.

"May I touch it?" Reagan reached a finger out to caress the muted black steel, but Chad pulled it away. "I won't break it, I assure you, Ms. Morgan."

Chad quirked an eyebrow and moved the gun closer to Reagan, giving her a dubious look. Perhaps it was just Reagan, but the electricity between them was sparking like a southern thunderstorm. She felt like her hair was standing on end as she leaned closer to Chad to stroke the gun. It was warm, but cool to the touch all at the same time. For some reason the thought of it being close to Chad's breast popped into Reagan's mind as she continued to run her finger down the barrel. *Lucky gun,* she thought. Turning towards Chad, she reached behind the woman to stabilize herself and realized she was leaning against Chad's arm. Chad's biceps rubbed between her breasts as she continued to stroke the gun with the tip of her finger.

"Does it have a lot of kick?" Reagan whispered into Chad's ear.

"Not much, being a semi-auto, the action of the slide moving to eject the round and chamber another helps eliminate some of the kick."

"Could I handle something that big?" Reagan whispered so close to Chad's ear she could smell Chad's scent. A musky, earthy scent, making Reagan think of things other than guns, roses, and white powder.

"Oh, I think you could handle this weapon without any issues."

"Perhaps, you'll give me a lesson?"

As Chad turned towards her, Reagan took advantage of the opportunity. Chad's arm moved just enough, brushing across her nipples, she moved closer and kissed Chad. Warm lips opened, inviting a response. Chad took the invitation, slipping her tongue in just deep enough that Reagan could taste the faint hint of alcohol. Leaving the warmth of the gun, Reagan worked her hand inside Chad's blazer and palmed her breast. Someone let out a moan only spurring the two women on further.

Running her hand across the hard nipple pressed against Chad's tight shirt, a jolt speared through her.

Reagan raked her nails across the front of the crisp white shirt and felt the nipple harden. Gently, she took the tip between her fingers and tugged on it. Reagan shifted around the front of Chad and straddled her hips, continuing her assault on Chad's mouth. Dueling tongues fought for control as Reagan felt Chad grip her hips and pull her closer. She heard the zipper of her dress and the cool blast from the air conditioner prickled her skin when Chad peeled the dress down off her shoulders.

Moving her lips across Chad's jaw to her ear, she ran her tongue around the lobe before nipping at it, her teeth grazing it. Chad's hips arched into hers. She continued her path down Chad's neck, alternating between sucking and nipping until finding Chad's sweet spot. Chad's fingers threaded through her hair, with a strong hand holding Reagan in place, sucking the throbbing vein and taut muscle of her neck. Arching her back, she pressed herself against Chad's thigh and slowly gyrated back and forth against the hard muscle beneath her. She kept the delicate pressure on her clit as she arched her hips further, making sure only her clit was engaged with Chad's thigh. She could feel the start of an orgasmic spasm so she slowed down, wanting to string it out as long as possible. Suddenly, she felt her breast fall forward when Chad unhooked her bra and slipped her dress down to her hips. The maddening dance between divesting each other of clothes and not wanting to break apart to do it only added to Reagan's fervor. She felt her hair pulled, arching her back as Chad's lips devoured one nipple and then the other.

Without warning, Chad flipped her on her back, stripped her dress down her thigh, and tossed it onto the other seat. As she wedged herself between Reagan's thighs, Reagan pushed her head down and lifted her hips. She was desperate for release and her orgasm was so close.

"Please," Reagan moaned. "Fuck me."

The darkness outside helped conceal the two women frantically pawing at each other. The air conditioning barely helped cool the sweat beading down Reagan's stomach when Chad flattened her tongue against her distended clit. The hard swipe of her tongue was replaced by a smooth, wet swirl as Chad's tongue danced around her clit, flicking it with each encounter. Reagan felt her lips parted and then Chad's tongue slid down to her wetness, poking it.

"Inside," Reagan commanded. "I want to feel you inside me."

The soft pressure against her opening increased as Chad slipped one, then two fingers into her, filling her. Slowly, with the thick pressure moving deeper into her, she tightened down on the hand, ready to come at any moment. Stealing herself, she wanted to hold-off the orgasm, to enjoy the pressure of Chad's body on hers for as long as possible. Chad's hand gripped her breast and squeezed the small mound, pushing her down so she could raise her hips. She drove her fingers into Chad's hair and pushed her head gently against her pussy, spurring her on. Reagan felt her hips begin to jerk as she held herself tighter against Chad's mouth.

"Oh, god," she squeezed out clenching her jaw.

The little hairs all over her body popped-up, signaling her impending orgasm, before it broke across her body. As if on cue, Chad worked her fingers faster, sliding in practically to her palm and back out again as her other hand slid down to Reagan's hip and held her tighter to her mouth. Bucking, Reagan could only focus on the tension coiling and releasing in her in multiple spasms. Her pussy milked Chad's fingers and kept its tight hold on them, as if begging for more, and Chad seemed quite willing to oblige the silent request.

Reagan pushed on Chad's head trying to release the hold she had on her. If she wasn't careful she could chase the orgasm longer, each stroke, each lick, pushing her further along her path of continuance, but eventually they would get caught and she wanted to feel Chad on her own tongue before she had the chance to say no.

"Please stop. I can't take anymore."

"Oh, but I think you can," Chad said swiping her tongue across the tendon next to Reagan's lips making her jerk. "See you're primed for more."

"That might be true, but—oh god. I want," Reagan broke off as another orgasm spasmed through her. "I—want to—God."

Reagan rose up on her elbows and scooted back slightly to emphasize her point. Raising Chad's face to hers, she kissed her, tasting herself on Chad's wet lips. Pulling Chad on top of her, she tugged at Chad's shirt.

"Off."

Yanking it up over Chad's head, she stopped its progress as Chad protested. Reagan wasn't about to be detoured from her destination. She let the shirt bind Chad's arms as she flipped Chad over on her back, attacking the bra covering her small breasts. Pulling the cups down she wrapped her lips around one of Chad's nipples and sucked while she tortured the other. Chad stopped struggling for a moment when Reagan raked her teeth over the tip.

"Stop struggling. Sit back and enjoy the equal treatment," Reagan commanded.

She let her tongue travel down the length of Chad's belly, trailing along the scar disappearing beneath Chad's pants. Unhooking the belt and opening the pants, she stopped her travels, and yanked at the tops of Chad's pants, jerking them to her knees. Naked! The scar stopped just above Chad's pubic bone. That's where Reagan began her journey again until reaching the tight bundle of curls surrounding what she wanted. Gently parting Chad's lips, Reagan let the tip of her tongue slip between them to work the hood of Chad's clit. Chad began to struggle with her shirt again and Reagan knew it wouldn't be long before she was free. Reagan went back to work before she was stopped permanently.

"Ms. Reynolds, please," Chad pleaded.

"Please what?"

Reagan ignored the pleadings and continued to work her tongue between Chad's now tightened thighs. Sucking the clit into her mouth, she moved back and forth over it as she grabbed Chad's ass and forced her farther up to gain better access to her destination. The more Chad jerked the more determined Reagan was to have what she wanted. Pushing her tongue deeper into the tight lips, she curved her tongue into Chad and flicked her clit faster. Without warning, she felt Chad jerk in her mouth as the ass in her hands tightened, paused, and then jerked again. Reagan waited and when there wasn't additional response, she crawled up Chad's torso, kissing and touching each scar that littered the beautiful body. After a few more well-placed kisses on Chad's nipples, she helped her pull down the dress shirt and smiled at the frowning face.

"What's good for the goose is good for the gander. Isn't that what they say?" Reagan laid her finger across Chad's lips before she could respond. "Clearly, we both want the same thing, so let's don't deny it. I won't lie, Chad. I'm very attracted to you and I would like to get to know you better, if you'll let me." Reagan knew she was making herself vulnerable, but right now she didn't care.

Chapter Nineteen

Chad had jerked her pants up, pissed that she had let her primal urges get the best of her. Reagan had flirted with her the whole night and she had let her control the situation. Now she had compromised her own position on the job. She could see Reagan was waiting for a response, but she couldn't give her what she wanted. Conveniently, the limo slowed to a stop. Within seconds the door swung open and Sophia popped her head in, announcing their arrival at the safe house.

Stepping out, she stormed past Sophia and barked an order, "Help, Ms. Reynolds out, please."

"You got it."

Chad pounded on the door and rushed past Marcus as he opened it. "Hey, how was dinner?"

"Fine, got anything new?" Chad asked, not really caring at the moment.

"As a matter of fact—"

"Can it wait? I need a shower. When I'm done, we'll chat. Oh, I'm changing the rotation and putting you in charge of Ms. Reynolds's daily care," Chad said, slamming the bedroom door behind her.

"You're the boss," Marcus said from behind the door.

Peeling off her gun harness and clothes, she stepped into a steaming hot shower, hoping to wipe away any traces of Reagan's mouth from her body. She had reacted so quickly, her body betrayed her at every level and she'd enjoyed it. She had compromised her position and her job. The only thing she could do now was turn it all over to Marcus, who would be able to view everything with a clear mind and heart.

"Fuck!" She slammed her fist against the tiles of the shower. How could she have been so stupid? Stepping out of the hot spray, she rubbed her skin, trying to alleviate the pain she had been oblivious to moments before. Reagan had gotten more than just under her skin, she had succeeded in getting into her head. Why didn't she stop Reagan when she pulled her shirt over her head? Why didn't she protest more? Reagan had taken control and she liked it—no, she enjoyed it. She was surprised she'd had the power to stop Reagan from continuing; she was damn near over the edge, hanging on by her fingertips before she pulled herself back. Her nerves were just at the surface and it wouldn't take much to bring out the bitch in her.

Yanking the towel, she accidently pulled the bar off the wall. It landed on the floor with a crash. "Great, now I'm breaking things."

"Chad?" A soft voice whispered through the door.

"Go away, Reagan."

"I'm not going away, Chad."

Chad wrapped the towel around her waist and put her hands on her hips. She was steaming mad, but it wasn't Reagan's fault. She only had herself to blame. Reagan didn't do anything to her that Chad hadn't let happen. Nevertheless, she'd fucked up the job. Literally.

"I always seem to catch you in the buff," Reagan said, emulating Chad's stance.

"Well if you respected the fact the door was closed, you wouldn't see me naked." Chad didn't move, why? Reagan had seen her, tasted her, and made her orgasm. What else was left. Her dignity?

"We need to talk."

"I think we're way past talking, don't you?"

"Perhaps, but I think we need to talk about what happened in the limo."

"What's happened has happened. Now we need to move on."

"So let me get this right. You're going to tell me what happened in the limo meant nothing to you?"

Chad flinched. Saying what happened in the limo meant nothing would clearly hurt Reagan. If they had met under different circumstances, they would have probably exchanged numbers, become acquainted, and probably had at least one date. The reality was she was paid to protect Reagan, not fuck her and doing so had just compromised her position.

"Marcus is taking over your daily protection."

"What?"

"You heard me. I've compromised the job and I'm taking a position in the rear of the operation."

"Are you saying that because you can't trust yourself to be around me, or because it meant something more to you, too?"

"Reagan, we hardly know each other."

"I see, so what happened in the limo was just sex."

"Not exactly."

"Then what exactly was it?"

Reagan stepped closer and Chad stepped back. "Don't."

"Don't what?"

Chad tried to step back again, but was stopped by the bed behind her. Reagan smiled and advanced closer. Looking down, she watched as Regan's warm hands grabbed her hips, pulling them tightly together. Trying to act unfazed, she stared over the top of Reagan's head. Then she felt Reagan's hand slide up her rib and stop just beneath her breast. Squeezing her eyes shut, she grabbed the advancing hand, but not before Reagan's other hand stroked down her scar and into her towel.

"Reagan," she whispered.

"Chad."

"We can't do this."

"We already have, besides didn't you just tell me you're not my bodyguard anymore?" Reagan stood on the tips of her toes and looked Chad in the eyes. "I think it changes things."

Before Chad could say anything she was lying on her back with Reagan firmly planted on top of her, straddling her hips, pulling the towel from between them. She felt awkward as her hands were pulled over her head, Reagan's breast directly over her mouth.

"I could easily get out of this Ms. Reynolds."

"Oh, it's Ms. Reynolds, now. I see."

As she opened her mouth to say something a nipple was dropped in. She did her best not to bite it as she began to speak, but the temptation was too overwhelming.

"Ouch!" Reagan pulled back and sat up, grabbing her breast. "You did that on purpose."

"Actually, I tried to tell you to stop, but it seems my mouth was filled with your breast."

As she tried to sit up, Reagan pushed her back on the bed. "Well, since you're so good with your mouth, Ms. Morgan, perhaps I can persuade you to continue."

"Reagan, I don't think this is a good idea."

"Funny, but I don't think I asked for your opinion."

Chad would not be controlled by a woman like Reagan again. Not unless she wanted it, and right now she wasn't in the mood. Rolling around on the bed, Chad tried to gain the upper hand but found herself twisted in the sheets. Cursing herself for not making the bed, she tried to unravel herself, but only succeeded in pulling them tighter around herself and Reagan. She felt fingers slip between her legs and Reagan's mouth on her now throbbing neck. Continuing to struggle was only adding to the tension between them and Chad could feel herself losing control once again as Reagan rubbed against her clit. Her body jerked against the constant motion. She arched her back and drove Reagan high between her legs. The added friction propelled her orgasm deeper as Reagan's hip rocked back and forth against her.

"Fuck."

❧ ❧ ❧ ❧

Once again, drops of water glistened on her lean body as she leaned on the dresser. Chad stared at her reflection in the mirror. She was starting to think the dark circles under her eyes were worth every minute Reagan had kept her up. The night before had left her weak-kneed, wanting. Reagan knew how to push all her buttons. Looking past her reflection, she spied Reagan's naked leg sticking out from under the covers on her bed.

What had she done? She hadn't just crossed the line, she had practically tripped on it as she jumped over it and back again. Then for good measure she crossed once more. Things had been said last night in lust she didn't expect Reagan to remember, but Chad did, and that was enough to tell her she needed to leave. She'd explain things to Marcus, since she hadn't had the chance last night. Throwing the few things she had unpacked back in her bag, thankful she never really unpacked anywhere, she dressed. Grabbing her shoulder harness, she walked into the bathroom, shut the door and pulled the slide to her automatic. It was loaded. Dropping the clip, she checked and then pushed it back into the gun. She sat on the toilet and looked down at the weapon in her hands. It had all started so innocently last night with her gun, and now she had Reagan all over her, in her, on her. Her mind was saturated with thoughts of Reagan lying naked in her arms, mewing out an orgasm.

Problems could easily be fixed, but this was more than a problem. This had moved to an impossible situation she must extricate herself from, now. Sliding the gun into its home, she snapped the trigger lock down and walked out into the darkened room. Once more, she took in Reagan's naked body lying on her bed and wished they had met under different circumstances. Reaching for her bag, she resisted leaning over and kissing the exposed foot. If she were lucky, she would never have to see Reagan Reynolds again before the job was over. It would be best for both of them. Reagan would only ask questions, want answers, and need more than she could give.

Slipping out the door, she silently shut it, but before she could move, she heard Marcus' deep voice.

"Leaving?"

"I'm glad you're not asleep. You're taking over her detail. I've compromised her safety, so I'll take rear op. I'll send in Thomas to help with rotation."

"What happened in the limo? Sophia said you practically knocked her down getting out and then you rushed in here. I haven't seen you until now."

"I fucked up, buddy." Chad sat down on the sofa and buried her head in her hands. "Big time."

"You mean you fucked her."

"Same thing."

"Look, it's been a long time since you've been with someone, it was bound to happen. Besides, you've been beating yourself up over Dawn for a long time. Don't you think it's time you stopped?"

Chad glared at Marcus. Dawn was her wife, the love of her life, and she hadn't been able to stop her suicide. She'd focused too much on work and had missed all the signs. Her mental illness had been progressing and Chad had conveniently missed it.

"You're treading on dangerous waters here, Marcus. You don't know what you're talking about, buddy." Chad's voice sounded more like a warning than friendly.

"Chad," Marcus sat next to her on the couch and put his hands together. "You didn't know. No one knew. Hell, her own mom didn't know. They talked every day and she didn't know how bad Dawn was, Chad."

"Back off, Marcus," her voice was menacing.

"I'm not backing off. If you want to take this outside and work some of it off, then I'm good, but I'm tired of seeing you all wrapped up over this. This shit needs to stop now. I don't know what happened in there tonight, but I have a pretty good idea and now you're running. So either she got to you, got you feeling something you thought had died with Dawn, or you're feeling guilty, either way you need to handle you're shit, Chad."

Without thinking, she threw a right hook, catching Marcus on the chin. "I told you to mind your own fucking business. Now take my advice before I fire you." Getting up, she stalked over to her bags and strode to the front door with one thought—run. "I'll call you when I get back to the office. Tell Ms. Reynolds about the staff changes and make sure you keep her safe. Someone still wants her dead and it's our job to see that doesn't happen." She turned back to Marcus and shook her head. "I'm sorry about your chin. Earlier, you said you had something, what was it?"

"You need to cool down first. It isn't something that can't wait, so I'll fax it to the office."

"I'll call later."

"Go home Chad. Get some sleep and handle your shit. Otherwise, you aren't gonna have a crew to worry about."

"Call and have them get the plane ready. I'll send Thomas back after he drops me off. Remember watch her like a hawk, Marcus."

"What if she asks about you?"

"Lie."

Chapter Twenty

"What do you mean she's gone? Where did she go?"

"She's handling rear operations. She's running a couple of leads back in California."

"Bullshit. I'm calling bullshit on that, Marcus."

"Either way, she isn't here. So I'm in charge." Flipping through the papers on his clipboard, he continued, "You have a ten o'clock and then lunch with Mr. Wilson, and then you have a two o'clock with—"

"I know my schedule, Marcus. I set it up."

"Yes, I know, but my job is to keep you on schedule. Sophia will be the one going with you to the meetings."

"Why?"

"She won't draw attention like I would. Remember, meat hanging around your neck? Someone is bound to notice my hulking ass. Everyone will assume she's just your assistant, but don't get cute. I don't want to have to hunt you down like Chad had to. Play nice with the team and this will go much smoother."

"I was playing nice," Reagan whispered low, walking towards her bedroom.

Just like that, Chad was gone. No explanation, no answers, no discussion. Throwing herself on her bed, she felt a little life drain out of her. Instead of waking up wrapped in a lover's arms, she woke to find herself cold and alone. *Why? I pushed too fast with Chad. That's why,* she chided herself. When she wanted something she went after it, no questions, no second thoughts— those were for wusses. She'd done it because she had been on a roller coaster and wanted company. Her solitary journey through life was finally wearing her down to the point where she was almost ready to toss in the towel. Screw the company, she would cash out and live as most of the wealthier women did. Shopping, lunching at the country club, tennis, or golf, she wasn't particularly good at either, and travel. Alone. Is that what she truly wanted? Grabbing her pillow tight, she buried her head in it and screamed, full throaty and wrenching. Her raw throat protested when she finally swallowed.

"Great, now I'll be hoarse, too."

Staring through the shear panels of the window dressing at nothing, her mind wandered, searching for answers to her out-of-control life. Was it worth it? Was all the skullduggery, the changing cars and moving locations worth it just to head Reynolds Holdings? What if she let someone else take the reins? Could that truly be the worst thing that could happen?

"Hell yes," she said, sitting up. "I won't see my father's hard work, his vision, and his ideas be screwed up by someone who only cares about the bottom line."

Chad had made her decision. As far as Reagan was concerned, she was just a hiccup in life, a diversion on her path. Now she would stay focused on the path set before her. CEO of Reynolds Holdings was her only goal; she would worry about happiness, marriage, and all those other things later. Right now, that meant working on the tasks at hand—board members and their votes. The line of succession was set. She was next in line and ready to take her rightful place at the head of the table.

Damned be Chad Morgan.

❧❧❧❧

"Ready, Marcus?"

"Actually, Ms. Reynolds, Sophia will be escorting you today."

"Fine, can we get going now?"

Reagan spied Sophia waiting patiently at the door. Her dress was impeccable, her demeanor calm, and she flashed her welcoming smile, in that patronizing way bodyguards placated their charges. It was going to be another long day, and she doubted there would be adult beverages and good food afterwards. Never mind the fact she was already wondering how Chad was fairing. Not her problem, she reminded herself. Chad was simply a nice diversion that had taken her leave. Walking out the door, she felt like the president, with people in what she could only assume were tactical positions.

"Stop!" Marcus said, standing dead still.

"What's wrong?"

"Sophia, take her back in the house now!"

Reagan looked around frantically, she didn't know what she was looking for, but something had spooked her protection team and now a cold shard cut threw her. Sophia grabbed her hand and jerked her to the front door. Within seconds they were in the house. Sophia stood over her, gun drawn, her eyes scanning the room and then focused on the door.

"What happened?"

"Marcus says jump, we jump."

"I see."

Reagan wrapped her arms around her briefcase and pulled it tightly against her chest. Hopefully, it would add a layer of protection, since she was sure she was the only one without body armor, a gun, or any other way to protect herself. That's what Chad was here for wasn't it? Oh wait, Chad wasn't here. She was off in the rear conducting some sort of operation or something.

"She ran!"

"What?"

"Chad, she ran." The realization suddenly hit Reagan.

"I'm sorry, Ms. Reynolds I don't know what you're asking." Sophia gave Reagan a puzzled look before turning her attention back to the door.

"Chad, she was afraid I was going to ask her about the scars on her chest. She was afraid I was going to put her in another inta—" Reagan stopped in mid-sentence suddenly realizing she was giving voice to her thoughts. "Nothing. Sorry, I'm just rambling."

Sophia's eyes seemed to relay an apology that should have come from Chad, but it hadn't. Instead she ran away from the inevitable questions she knew would come from someone she had just made love to, well had sex with, twice in less than twelve hours.

"How fucked up is this?"

"Ms. Reynolds?"

"Oh nothing, I'm just thinking out loud. Sorry," she said, waving off Sophia.

A soft knock on the door brought Sophia to a standing position, aiming her weapon at the door. Two more knocks and Sophia was peeking through the viewfinder. Moving to the side, she reached across her body and opened the door, pointing her gun at head height.

"Whoa there, just me. We're ready. Let's go, Ms.

Reynolds."

Reagan sat firmly rooted in place, staring at Marcus. "I'm not moving until you tell me what happened out there."

"It isn't anything for you to worry about. I've cleared the vehicle and we're ready to roll."

"Nice try, but try again."

"Ms. Reynolds," Marcus stressed her last name. It was clear he wasn't in the mood for any insubordination, but she wasn't his peer, she was the client and she wasn't about to move without know what happened outside. She was becoming more paranoid with each passing day.

"I asked you a question, Marcus. I'm not trying to be difficult, but I won't be kept in the dark either. What happened out there?" The tremor was evident in her voice.

Looking at Sophia and back to Reagan, he cleared his throat and handed her a clear plastic bag with something in it. At first she couldn't make out what it was, until she turned it over and saw the writing on the paper. Another death threat was clearly scribbled across the torn sheet of yellow ruled paper.

"You thought you were safe, but you're not. Die Bitch!!!!!" She felt the color drain from her face and a cold sweat sprouted all over her body. "Well, I guess they mean business with all those exclamation marks," she tried to joke, but knew she fell short when no one, including herself, laughed.

"I'll call, Chad and let her know about this," Marcus said, taking the protected evidence.

"How did they find me? I thought this was a safe house."

Marcus looked at Sophia, who could only shrug

her shoulders. "I don't know, Ms. Reynolds, but I can tell you we'll find out who did this. We're going to have to move again."

"Great. Are you kidding me?"

"I don't kid, Ms. Reynolds. I'll have Thomas pack your things when he gets here and we'll change locations."

"I'm not canceling my meetings, so don't ask."

"Ms. Reynolds—"

"Don't, just don't. I have to handle my business and this is more important than ever. So, deal with it. If you do your job, then I'm safe. If you don't, then it won't matter what I do," she said, feeling less brave than she hoped it sounded.

"Like I said, I'll call Chad. Okay?" Marcus said looking around the room. "We'll get this stuff packed up and ready to roll. I'll be back with Thomas and we'll change locations. Ms. Reynolds, please don't give Sophia any problems today, we need you onboard."

"I understand." She looked at Sophia. "If you're ready, we really do need to go."

Reagan felt as if she had six sets of legs walking to the car. Sophia and Marcus were so close she could practically feel the heat of their bodies assaulting her. Scared wouldn't begin to describe how she was feeling. The thought that someone had found out where she was just after switching locations was disturbing. Whoever was behind all of this wasn't going to win, they weren't going to make her change her mission, period. She stood straighter and walked with purpose to the limo. How could Chad have left when things were so—off-kilter?

She slid into the limo, followed by Sophia. Enclosure in the steel casing didn't seem to calm her, instead she was starting to feel like she did in the elevator yesterday.

"Um, I hate to be a bother, but do we have any water? I'm starting to feel—"

"Ms. Reynolds, you don't...."

Chapter Twenty-one

The phone call from Sophia was frantic. Whoever was behind the death threats had found Reagan and now she was in a hospital. Nothing serious, minor exhaustion probably brought on by stress, the doctor said. They were going to keep her overnight for observation because of the attempted poisoning and now the fainting.

"Great," Chad said jumping up from her seat and sending it careening across the office. Somebody, somehow, had found out where they had taken Reagan, but how? Marcus had checked her bags, they had the agency locate the safe house for them so they were off the radar, but they had found out somehow. Pulling her cell phone, she hit speed dial and waited.

"Marcus, how is she?" She listened while he explained the details from the doctor and the changes he had made. "I'm on my way back. I'll meet you at the hospital. Yes, I'm sure. I should've never left in the first place. Besides, I'm just in the way here. Rita's got everything under control," she said, looking over at Rita, who was busy scanning some reports that had just come in. "Yeah, see you in a couple of hours."

"Rita, what am I missing?"

Rita didn't look up from her report. "I don't know, Chad. I've gone through the background checks. I've re-checked their personal information, their bank info, and their personal lives. I can't find one damn thing within the organization."

"There has to be something we're overlooking."

"Maybe it's someone outside the company. Everyone inside is lily-white, I mean they are almost too squeaky clean."

"Okay, let's take two steps out from the inner circle of Reynolds Holding employees. Look at their friends, their family, anyone who might listen to the rants of a pissed off employee."

"You got it, but it's going to take some time."

"Yeah, I know, so put a rush on it. Call me when you find out anything, no matter how small the detail."

Chad picked up her bag. She hadn't even had a chance to stop at her place to unpack. Lucky for her.

❧ ❧ ❦ ❦

She watched Reagan sleeping and wondered if the woman dreamed. Chad had met women wound so tight they were almost ready to self-combust at the slightest tilt of their world. Reagan had more than rolled with the punches; she had landed on her feet ready to take on the next problem. That was something impressive in Chad's book. Settling herself in for a long night, Chad took out her tablet and began working through some ideas she'd had on the plane. If someone wanted Reagan dead, why not just kill her? They were close enough each time to do some serious damage, if not eliminate her. The more Chad thought about it the more she wondered if they were just playing a perverted game of cat and mouse with a different prize and a different goal in mind. Rita had uploaded all the employee files and had sent the files of those two-steps out from those employees, while she was off-loading at the airport. So now was a perfect time to go through them all.

Swiping through the pages, nothing out of the ordinary caught her eye. No firings, no credit deficiencies, hell there wasn't really even a parking ticket to speak of. Maybe that was the problem. The files were too clean, as Rita had said earlier. Almost like someone had scrubbed them clean. Going through the employee pictures wasn't any help either. Each photo showed employees in the standard issue Reynolds Holdings badge, smiles plastered over their faces. Nothing. Marcy's picture popped up on her screen. Chad noticed her smile lacked the warmth of the other employees. There was something Reagan had said at dinner, but what was it? Chad tried to remember, drumming her fingers on the arm of the chair. A baby or something? No, it was more than that. She had dated Reagan. Chad frowned while she stared at the picture, wondering what someone like Reagan saw in the plain-Jane, Marcy. Safe was the only word Chad could come up with. Marcy was safe, she wasn't a lesbian, and so there was no implied contract with a gal who sat on both sides of the fence. It had been Chad's experience, women who dabbled rarely stayed with it. Fluid or not, you either loved women and couldn't see yourself with the other gender, or you didn't. It was as easy as that for Chad.

Chad studied the picture. She got a weird vibe about Marcy. Something wasn't quite right. She had felt it when she sat in Frank's office and now she was feeling it again. The eyes, the eyes always gave the secrets away and Marcy's looked like they had a secret or two hiding behind them. Chad wrote down some notes for herself, closed her notebook, and stuffed it back into the inside pocket of her blazer. Something was off, but it would have to wait until later. Her brain was swimming right now, so she swiped her screen again and tried to read the latest headlines from around the world.

"Did someone piss in your cereal this morning?"

Chad heard Reagan's soft whisper, but couldn't see past the glare of her computer screen.

"No, why?"

"Oh, you just looked like you had something bad in your mouth."

"How're you feeling?"

"Fine, I don't know why they insisted on keeping me overnight."

"Well maybe it had something to do with the fact you've fainted twice in less than twenty-four hours and before that you ingested some nasty stuff."

"Hmmph," Reagan said, sitting up and tucking the sheets around her. "If it's all the same to you, I think I'd rather go home now."

"You could have denied the doctor's help at any time, Reagan. You and I both know, so don't act like someone forced you to stay."

Looking away, Reagan said, "Yeah, well I guess I was a little worried."

"I'm glad to hear you're taking this serious." Chad stood and stretched her arms over her head and yawned.

"So?"

"So, what?"

"So, tell me what happened."

"With?"

"Let's don't play coy, Chad," Reagan locked eyes

with her. "Why run?"

"I had work back at the office," Chad lied. She knew what Reagan meant, but wasn't ready for a come-to-jesus moment quite yet.

"I'm calling bullshit,"

"Bullshit?"

"Yeah, bullshit," Reagan said defiantly.

"Well not very professional, or lady-like are you?" Chad smiled trying to lighten the mood.

"Is that your style to fuck and run?"

"Look, Reagan, we can talk about this later. Right now you need to sleep."

Chad could feel Reagan amping up. Her posture went rigid and she didn't take her eyes off her as Chad walked around the cramped room. Slipping her tablet into her briefcase and putting it on the floor, Chad put her hands on her hips and looked right at Reagan. It would probably have been easier to intimidate if she hadn't slept with Reagan, but what was done, was done. Now, she had to take control of the situation or crazy could run deep and quick if she wasn't careful. Women could be unpredictable and Chad wasn't prepared if Reagan went sideways.

"If we were some place more private, we could have a conversation about what's happened in the last twenty-four hours, but we aren't." Chad moved closer and lowered her voice. "I don't plan on exposing my private life or yours to the hospital staff. Now, if you can't understand, then I'm sorry, but I'm kinda funny that way."

Reagan stood, pulling the IV stand as she walked towards Chad. She noticed the barely-there hospital gown was tied in the front affording Reagan some dignity, but Chad could only smile as Reagan grasped the front as it started to slip off her shoulder.

"Look," she said, throwing her hands up to stop Reagan. "Why don't you sit back down and relax? This can wait."

"What are you afraid of, Chad?"

"I'm not afraid of anything, Reagan. I just don't think this is the time or place for a discussion about what happened last night."

"Well, I do. So, you can either leave or get comfortable because we are going to have a talk," Reagan said, leaning against the bed.

Chapter Twenty-two

R eagan was hurt and feeling vulnerable as she waited for Chad to leave, which she suspected would happen any minute. The last few days had her feeling weak, scared, and excited all on one roller coaster of a ride. Reagan wasn't exactly accustomed to dealing with those feelings. Her life consisted of the standard level path that rarely deviated from the course she had succinctly set for herself. No highs, or lows and if the once-in-a-while sexcapade blew up in her face, so be it. She could handle it because she knew it was coming. Now she felt like the slightly out-of-control woman who just had the most mind-blowing sex of her life and wanted more. There was only one problem. Chad was the other woman and she didn't seem as though she was interested in extending the relationship past last night.

"Whatever you say, don't tell me last night was a mistake."

"I wasn't going to say that, but I'm still not comfortable talking about what happened here."

"I don't see anyone else here, do you?"

"No, but—"

"Good, sit," Reagan commanded. "Why? Why did you run?"

"Reagan—"

"Look, I've given this a lot of thought and I'm ready to check out and go home to California. You'll be relieved to know I'm ending your job effective immediately." Reagan rolled her eyes away from Chad effectively dismissing her.

She decided to take back control of a situation which had obviously gotten out hand. Her head hurt, her mind wandered, and she felt like shit. She wasn't in the mood for an argument, and it was clear Chad wasn't in the mood to talk rationally about the amazing sex they had shared. No, Chad was too busy hiding from her ghosts, or whatever kept her closeted away from the real world. Running was just her modus operandi when faced with a difficult situation, at least according to how Dr. Reagan saw things. God knows she had been in enough therapy to see all the signs. Wishing she were wrong would only open Reagan up to hurt, and denial wasn't something she practiced on a regular basis. Therefore, confronting Chad was the only way to put it all in a nice little neat package that could be stored away and not added as baggage to her already complicated life.

Chad sat motionless, as if waiting for a pseudo shoe to drop. She was going to be disappointed, because causing a scene over a lover wasn't Reagan's style. Lovers caused a scene over her and not the reverse. Reagan exhaled and tried to relax the stress piling on her shoulders.

"Have you talked to your father about your decision?"

"I tried, but Marcy said he went home early. He wasn't feeling well today."

"Really?"

"Probably stress. I'll call him in the morning and let him know to expect me tomorrow afternoon." Reagan sat back on the bed, suddenly tired and ready to call it a day. Clearly, Chad wasn't going to give her the courtesy of an answer to her questions, and right now, she didn't seem to care. "Now, if you don't mind, I'm feeling tired, suddenly." Reagan rolled over, tucked the thin sheets and blanket around her and sighed. Chad intrigued her, but she wasn't ready to sort through her baggage to expose the real woman. She had bigger battles to fight, like taking over the company. Focus, she told herself. A good fighter knew when to let the battle end and focus on the war.

"I'm not easy to get rid of Reagan." Chad settled into the uncomfortable chair.

"If only." Reagan said smugly. "Look, you win. You get to keep your secrets, your scars, and a couple of easy rolls-in-the hay. So why don't you be a good girl and go home? I'm not in the mood for a fight."

Reagan's body tensed with the lie. Maybe the nurse could give her something to help her sleep. She needed that more than she needed anything Chad could give her. Push-me, pull-me was how Reagan referred to what was happening between them. Great sex, but once it was over the push-away started. Pressing the call button, Reagan waited.

"Yes, Ms. Reynolds?" the soft voice said on the other end.

"Is this Ms. Channing?" Reagan's voice sounded flirty as she purred into the box.

"Yes, what can I get you, Reagan?"

"I can't seem to sleep. I was wondering if the doctor had prescribed something?"

"Let me talk to the doctor and see what she wants to do. I'm sure she would want you to sleep. If not I'll stop by and see if some hot tea or warm milk will work." The nurse flirted back.

"Thank you Ms. Channing."

"Of course."

The light went off and Reagan sighed again. If Chad had gone she would find a way to sleep, but since her bodyguard hadn't left yet, she would have to make do with a little flirting.

"You can go, Chad. You'll be safe and sound in California, but I'm still on the job."

The darkness of the room and Chad's new location in the corner kept Reagan from seeing her face, but she could hear her slow, methodical breathing. She knew Chad was staring directly at her, she could feel it. The problem was, instead of feeling relieved, her body ached for her touch. Wound tight, Reagan's heart raced and she tried to will it to slow down. Something about Chad always had her wishing for more—more touching, more answers, more...

"Ms. Reynolds, the doctor said you could take this." Nurse Channing walked into the room and touched the light pad next to Reagan's bed. "It's a sleeping pill. It should give you a few hours of uninterrupted sleep." She handed the paper cup to Reagan. "Or, I could help in another way, if you'd like."

Reagan smiled as the nurse touched her wrist and looked down at her watch. A tingle, flirted its way throughout her body as she looked at the young, innocent face smiling back at her. The scrubs hid what Reagan was sure was a young, nubile body.

"Well, I would love to have something non-narcotic, but I don't think I should."

"Well your pulse says something else, Ms. Reynolds."

"Oh, really?" Reagan toyed with the young woman. She knew Chad was watching intently and could hear every word between them. "How fast is it?"

"If I didn't know better, I would say you've just preformed a very strenuous exercise and I'm sure you haven't been out of this bed."

"No, I've been right here, being a good little girl."

"How good?"

"Very."

"Could you sit-up please?" the nurse said, pulling the stethoscope from around her neck. "I need to take your vitals."

"Of course."

"Could you open your gown so I can listen to your chest?"

Reagan undid the top tie of her gown and looked directly at Chad. The cold pad of the scope made her jerk.

"I'm sorry, I should have warmed this up."

Moving the stethoscope from the right side to the left, the nurse accidently brushed across Reagan's nipple, making it hard. Reagan closed her eyes and bit her lower lip as the nurse moved the device between her breasts and asked her to cough. Reagan gave the weakest cough she could and then took a deep breath sitting straight up. As the nurse moved to Reagan's back, she accidently—or purposely—slipped the gown off of her shoulder and began her routine again.

"Cough."

Again, Reagan gave a weak, barely audible cough. She was enjoying the show put on at Chad's expense. Chad's eyes never left hers, as Reagan watched an eyebrow shoot up in question. Smiling, she looked down at her bare breast and then back at Chad, this time with a smirk on her face.

"Well, everything looks good from here." The nurse picked up her chart and made some notes. "I'll need to take your blood pressure and then we're all done."

"Of course," Reagan said, pulling her arm from the gown, baring her chest, and extending it out for the cuff.

"So Ms. Reynolds, do you get to De Moines often?"

"Not as often as I like."

The nurse slid Reagan's arm between her arm and her body, caressing it as she did. She tightened the blood pressure cuff around Reagan's biceps, and then traced a line over her shoulder smiling at Reagan reassuringly.

"That's too bad."

"It is, isn't it?"

"You're very attractive, Ms. Reynolds, if you're staying on for a few more days, perhaps you'd like to get coffee or—something."

"The *or something* sounds intriguing." Reagan flashed her biggest smile. "Perhaps when I'm in town again we could do something?"

"I'll leave my number on the stand. Call me." The nurse finished her notes, removed the cuff, and pulled the gown over Reagan's arm. "I'll be back in a couple of hours to check on you, or if you need me for anything, just push the button. My shift ends in a couple of hours."

"I'll do that." Reagan grabbed the nurse's hand as it slid down her arm. "I might need help bathing later."

"Yes, you might, especially after taking that sleeping pill." Ms. Channing smiled. "Good night."

"Good night," Reagan said, watching the nurse leave.

"Was that necessary?"

☙ ☙ ☙ ☙

Chad tingled as she watched the nurse slide her hand up Reagan's arm and around her shoulder. She half-expected the woman to fondle Reagan's exposed breast right there in front of her. The anticipation shot a charge right through her, as she watched the whole seduction take place. She knew she could have made her presence known, but then again so could Reagan. Clearly, Reagan was toying with her.

She watched Reagan stretch and moan, letting the gown purposefully fall from her breast as she moved. The erect nipple caught Chad's attention as Reagan ran a hand over it, before covering it with her gown. Chad pulled on the legs of her slacks trying to ease the contact they were making with her clit. When that didn't work, she stood and wrestled them down, eliminating the stimulation.

"Going somewhere?" Reagan smiled.

"No, just stretching."

"I'm sorry, did I embarrass you when my breast was exposed?"

"Not at all. I've seen them before, and now the nurse has, too."

Chad heard a hint of jealousy ring through her snarky reply, but she didn't care. She knew Reagan pushed her buttons on purpose and it aggravated her that she felt it. Seeing how Reagan's body responded to the accidental touch of the nurse made Chad's body temperature spike. She felt like a voyeur as the two women flirted back and forth, almost culminating that banter with a possible encounter. The scene made Chad wet. She had to admit it turned her on and now she was ashamed of the fact that Reagan could affect her that way. She needed space from the temptress acting so innocent in the hospital bed. Otherwise, she might be all over her again.

"I'm going to get some coffee, can I bring you anything?"

"No, I'll probably be asleep when you get back, so if you want to leave, feel free." Reagan tied the strings to the top of the gown and rolled over, effectively dismissing Chad. Pushing the door open, Chad practically bumped into the nurse from earlier.

"Pardon me," Chad said, seizing the opportunity to size up the petite nurse.

"I'm sorry, I didn't see you go in."

"I'm not surprised, you were a little busy."

At least she has the decency to act embarrassed, Chad thought and held the door open for the woman. She watched her peer into the room and then back at Chad. "Where were you in there the whole time?"

Chad quirked an eyebrow and smiled devilishly, then walked away. She'd said all she needed to and now she left the nurse wondering if Chad would report her or not. It wasn't Chad's style to shred another person's career, not if they weren't part of her investigation. Plus, Reagan had led the nurse on. By no fault of her own, she had practically succumbed to Reagan's charms. Poor thing, she just doesn't know what she just avoided, thought Chad as she overshot the coffee cup she was holding and poured coffee down her slacks.

"Shit." She jerked back.

Chapter Twenty-three

Hi Dad. I tried reaching you at the office, but Marcy said you were still home sick. Are you okay?"

"I'm fine, honey. I'm sure it's just stress. So, what's this I hear that you are coming home and dismissing your protection detail? The threat is still out there, Reagan."

"I know, Dad. The meeting is in a couple of weeks and I've talked to enough board members that I think we're solid." Reagan looked over at Chad, who was working on her computer, obviously trying not to listen. "I thought I'd stay home and take some R&R." Reagan heard her father coughing and gasping for breath. "Dad, are you okay? You don't sound so good. I think you need to get to the hospital."

"I'm fine, Honey. It's just the flu or something. If I don't feel better in the morning, I'll see the doctor, I promise."

"I'll stop by on the way home and check on you."

"No, I'm good, just go home and get some rest yourself. You've been through enough. I'm a grown man. I can take care of myself. Marcy dropped off some homemade chicken soup. I'll eat some of that and then I'm going to bed."

"Okay, but if you need anything call me,

promise?"

"I promise."

Boarding the plane, Reagan said goodnight and did as the flight attendant instructed, turning her phone off and tossing it in her briefcase. She was worried about her father. He was the picture of health and rarely sick. Regardless of what he said, she was going to stop by and see him on her way home. That was all there was to it as far as she was concerned. Leaning her head back, she closed her eyes and sighed. Life suddenly had become complicated. Her attraction to Chad had taken a turn she didn't expect and the reality that someone wanted her dead screwed with her head.

"You're dad's sick?"

"Yeah," she said without opening her eyes. "He said it's probably stress."

"Hmm."

"You don't think it's stress?"

"Maybe."

Reagan looked at Chad, puzzled. "Is there something you're not telling me?"

"I'm not a doctor, so I wouldn't know what's wrong with your father."

"But you're not convinced he's sick."

"No, I believe him when he says he's ill." Chad shifted nervously in her seat, making Reagan wonder if she was hiding something from her.

"What aren't you telling me, Chad?" Reagan studied Chad's face for answers. "Why do I feel like you're hiding something from me?" Looking her in the eyes, Reagan wanted to shake her if it would make her talk, but she doubted anything would. If the connection of intimacy during sex didn't make for good pillow talk with Chad, then nothing would probably part those lips. "I would die if something happened to my father. He's all I have left." Reagan turned away and stared out into the empty sky, feeling the same emptiness in her heart.

"You'd survive, Reagan. You're a strong woman."

"Is that what you think? It's all about survival of the fittest? We all need someone, Chad. A parent, a lover, or friends, we all need that special connection to something or someone bigger than us."

"Maybe, maybe not."

It suddenly hit Reagan like a ton of bricks. "How long has she been gone?"

"Who?" Chad's eyebrows knitted together.

"The woman in the picture. How long have you two been broken-up?"

"We didn't break-up. Dawn committed suicide two years ago."

Reagan froze at the revelation. Suicide. She reached out to grab Chad's hand before she could shrink back from her touch. "I'm sorry, Chad. I had no idea, I—I mean—I just, I guess I don't know what to say."

"You don't have to say anything," Chad said, pulling her hand from Reagan's. "It was a long time ago and I've dealt with it. So you see, you can survive anything, if you're strong enough."

"I'm not sure I could be that strong," Reagan whispered, clutching the sudden pain in her heart. She'd never met anyone touched by suicide. She just couldn't imagine the pain Chad must have, or maybe still was going through. The photo on the dresser made sense now. Shaking her head she realized how crass she had been the other day when she picked it up and nonchalantly asked who it was, as if it mattered. Now, she wished she could take it all back. The snarky remarks, the way she had treated Chad from the start, and the sex. Okay, maybe not the sex, but at least the way she had thrown herself at Chad with little regard for her feelings.

"Don't do that."

"Do what?"

"Don't throw me a pity party in your head. I don't need it, so stop it right now."

Chad's look told Reagan everything she had thought was clearly written all over her face. How could she not feel pity for Chad? Her girlfriend had killed herself and Chad probably carried it around like an anchor around her heart, pulling her down.

"I'm sorry. I wish I could say I know what you're going through, but I would be lying."

"Don't worry, I'm a big girl, and I can handle my business." Chad's bravado was as false as the smile she usually had plastered on her face.

"What was she like?" Reagan asked.

"Who? Dawn?"

"Yeah, what was she like?" Reagan watched as Chad pulled on the seams of her pants and straightened out her legs. Clearly, she didn't want to talk about Dawn, but Reagan was genuinely interested in who could capture Chad's attention enough to capture her heart. The quiet in first-class replaced the mindless banter that had filled the cabin earlier. Studying Chad, Reagan wished she could just wrap her arms around her and hold her, rock her, tell her everything was going to be fine and time would heal the scars Dawn's suicide had left behind. All platitudes that rang hollow for a woman like Chad, who had a soul of cold steel. At least that was what she presented to the outside world. She was someone who fended off danger the way some people consumed lattes, on a daily basis.

Reagan felt the wall go up before she even looked at Chad. She appeared more uncomfortable than Reagan had ever seen her. Her mind tried to wrap itself around the idea of suicide. What went through a person's mind in those last minutes? Knowing that they would leave this earth, and those they loved behind to grieve such an awful, awful tragedy.

"Tell me one thing about her?"

"Why?"

"Because believe it or not, I care about you." Reagan hoped the sincerity of her voice was evident.

"She was unpredictable," Chad said, crossing her arms and resting her head against the backrest.

"Drinks?" The flight attendant said, breaking the tension between the two.

"Rum and coke." Chad ordered without opening her eyes.

"Whiskey, neat." That got Chad's attention, and she looked over at Reagan. "Surprised? I like a good stiff drink every once in a while." Reagan smiled and patted Chad's hand. "So, why unpredictable? Explain."

"She always had me guessing. I never knew which Dawn I was going to find when I got home. Happy, depressed, funny, I just never knew."

"Was she always like that?"

"Not always, not until the last few months."

"What happened?"

"She was diagnosed with bipolar disorder. When she was up, she was up, when she swung the other way, she was depressed. Simple as that."

"Mental illness isn't as simple as that, Chad. I'm

sure in your business you've experienced a few people you would categorize as mental cases." Reagan could hear the pain in Chad's voice. Clearly, she hadn't gotten over Dawn's suicide. The wounded look on her face more evidence that she wasn't as good at hiding her feelings as Reagan had thought. Reagan hesitated asking the next question, not sure if Chad would continue being candid with her, but what the hell, the job was over and she had nothing to lose. "When did it all start?"

❧❧❧❧

Chad tried to rub the tension out of the tight muscles in her neck. She hadn't talked about Dawn in at least a year and she wasn't sure she wanted to now. Reagan's gentle prodding made her feel vulnerable, weak, and lost somewhere in Dawn's memory. Dawn was the love of her life, the light in her dark soul, and she blamed herself every day for her death.

"I don't know. One day things just went south. She had to stop working in the office, she lost her motivation for the job, she said."

Looking back, it had been such a gradual process that Dawn had dismissed any of Chad's concerns. Slowly, Chad gave Reagan the reader's digest version of what had happened, not too much, but just enough to satisfy her curiosity. Time hadn't smoothed out the rough edges of those memories and Chad doubted it ever would.

Reagan cupped her chin and turned Chad's face towards hers. "It wasn't your fault, I know you feel that way now, but trust me, you didn't do this to her."

"What do you know about it?" Chad's snarky

reply slipped out.

"I blamed myself for my mom's death for most of my life. That's what I know about losing someone and thinking you had something to do with it," Reagan whispered.

Chad felt like someone had just kicked her in the gut. She had forgotten about Reagan's mom dying during childbirth and could only imagine the guilt that came with it.

Lifting Reagan's chin, she looked into soft eyes, wishing she could take back the hurt she'd put there. Her rough edges were showing again and she mentally kicked herself for being so brash.

"You're right, I'm sorry. I forgot about how your mother died."

Warm breath caressed Chad's lips as Reagan moved closer. Soft, warm, and inviting was how the kiss started, but passion pushed through and Chad found herself devouring Reagan's mouth. Threading her fingers through soft locks, she turned Reagan's head to the right and slowly kissed her way down Reagan's neck. The flame that started with the kiss was burning its way down her body, setting her on fire.

"Chad."

Chad worked her mouth over the throbbing pulse, sucking on it gently at first and then raking it with her teeth. Her need overtook her mind and she was almost past a point of return.

"Chad." Reagan pulled back, breathless. "Chad, we're in first-class, not exactly a private room." Reagan stroked Chad and searched her face. "Trust me, if we were alone, it would be a different story,"

"I'm sorry, I don't know what I was thinking," Chad said, dropping her icy exterior back in place.

"Don't. Don't do that, Chad."

"What?"

"Don't act like that meant nothing to you. I'm not stupid. I can see how your body is reacting. God, you would have to be blind to miss it."

Her head was spinning, she didn't do emotional well, and it was just easier for her to shut it down and motor through it all. It was why she ran away from Reagan the night before. Swallowing hard, she tried to center herself before she said something she would regret later. Her body was firing off every nerve pulsing through it. She had come to expect that kind of reaction when it came to Reagan and now she had admit she was starting to like the feeling.

"I'm sorry, you're right."

"I'm right, as in you do feel something for me, or I'm right, you're shutting down and getting ready to run again?"

"Yes."

"Oh geez, to use your words on you - don't make me flirt this out of you." Reagan sat back, frustrated.

Chad squeezed the hand she was still holding, trying to calm Reagan down. The last thing she needed was a scene on the plane and an air marshal to come running to help. Control, it was what she did best.

"You're correct. I ran the other night. You're the first woman I've been with more than one time since Dawn. Obviously, you've seen the way I've looked at you, and then the other night when I was massaging you I could feel—"

"Wait, what? You were the one?" Reagan moved her hands back and forth, mimicking a massaging motion. "You're the one who had your hands all over, I mean—you oiled my...."

"Yes."

"Oh, Christ."

"I didn't hear you complaining. In fact, I think you said I had great hands, if my memory serves me right."

Reagan blushed at the implications and Chad thought it was sexy as hell. She knew Reagan would be rethinking the whole massage, wondering what she had said. It didn't matter, her job was almost over and chances were pretty good she wasn't going to see Reagan again.

"I'm sorry to intrude, but the captain has turned on the seatbelt sign. We're on our final approach to San Jose."

"Thanks." Chad let go of Reagan's hand and buckled herself in. A couple more hours and we'll go our separate ways, she thought.

"Don't think this conversation is over," Reagan patted Chad's hand and whispered. "I'm not done with you."

Great.

Chapter Twenty-four

I'd like to go by my father's house before you drop me off," Reagan said as she slipped into the back of the SUV.

"No problem." Chad shook Marcus's hand as he approached. "Hey, buddy. Did you check out that information I gave you?"

Marcus leaned down and whispered in Chad's ear. "Can I talk to you in private for a moment?"

Glancing over at Reagan, Chad had a feeling this wouldn't be news she wanted to share, if her suspicions were correct. Nodding her head towards the back of the SUV, she motioned to Sophia to load the bags in the back.

"I'll be right back," she told Reagan.

"Okay."

"What's up?"

"I think Reagan has a little brother."

"What?"

Marcus nodded, affirming what he'd said. "Yep, when you said that secretary had an affair with Reagan, it got me thinking. So, I did a little digging. It seems the office assistant had an affair with dad, too."

"Reagan never said anything about Marcy being a ladder-climber."

"Maybe she doesn't know."

"What makes you think Frank is the father and why didn't he say anything to Reagan?"

"Maybe he doesn't know?"

"Doesn't know?"

"It's pretty twisted. I've got Rita working on a lead, but if I'm right, I don't think Marcy told anyone. Seems she took a leave of absence to take care of a sick mother and had the kid in another state."

"How'd you find out about the affair?"

"It wasn't easy, but her sister let it slip when I went out and interviewed her."

"How could we have missed this little tidbit of information?"

"No one was talking and Reagan didn't know. Nice little family secret that even the family doesn't know about." Marcus looked inside the SUV. "Enough motive for attempted murder? What do you think she's going to say when she finds out?"

Chad jutted her chin out and stretched her neck, a reaction to frustration that she seemed to do often lately. Following Marcus's gaze, she wondered what Reagan would do if it was true.

"Are you sure the boy's Frank's?"

"We don't have DNA evidence, if that's what you're asking. I'm trying to track down the birth certificate as we speak, but look, if Reagan was out of the way, then the kid becomes the heir-apparent, and by default, Marcy."

"That's a lot to suppose, my friend."

"You got a better reason for all of this?"

Chad wished she had, but she had seen people do far worse for fewer gains. Chad's mind began to race at all the possibilities. If Marcy were behind the death threats, Chad would need to tread carefully and not accidentally show her hand. The sad part was there was a child in the middle of all of this and a dad who didn't know he had a son out there somewhere. What about Reagan? How would she handle the news that she had a little brother? Chad knew one thing for certain: Frank had to tell Reagan about the possibility of a brother, not her.

"Okay, keep working on that lead and let's get some answers, quick. I don't like the fact that we still don't know who's behind all of this and now there might be an innocent boy involved."

"Will do."

"Thanks, buddy."

Chad slid into the front seat and shut the door. Normally, she would have sat next to the client for protection, but her mind was whirling with all the possibilities, and the last thing she needed was for Reagan to distract her with a simple touch.

"Are you ready to see your dad?"

※ ※ ※ ※

The winding driveway was dark and the outside lights barely lit the huge, manicured yard as they pulled around the circular drive. The porch lights were blazing though. *At least someone has some common sense,* Chad thought, looking around the compound.

"You're dad lives well, for someone who lives alone."

She looked back at Reagan, who was studying the house. "Yeah, it's the family home. I don't think he could part with it when my mom died. Too many good memories, he said."

"Hmm. I don't see any lights on. Does he go to bed early?"

"Not normally. He gets maybe five hours of sleep

a night, so he's always up late."

"Maybe he went to bed early 'cause he's sick?"

"No, he knew I would come by." Reagan pulled keys from her purse.

"But he told you not to."

"He knows I would stop by anyway. Look, if you want to sit in the car while I check on him, that's fine. Just stop with the stupid back-and-forth. Geez."

Chad could feel the tension rolling off Reagan. If she was worried earlier, the phone call didn't help matters. She'd been quiet during the ride from the airport and Chad practically had to pry what she wanted for dinner out of her. Reagan had slammed her food down so fast that Chad was sure she would have the worst case of heart burn later. Walking around the car, she opened the door and helped her out, before reaching into her jacket to unsnap the holster.

"Is that really necessary?"

"You didn't have a problem with my gun a couple of days ago," Chad said, smiling as she took Reagan's elbow and walked her to the door.

"Whatever."

Approaching the door, Chad looked around as she always did, scanning for anything out of the ordinary. Nothing seemed out of place. In fact, it was spotless. No shoes or newspapers were outside. The painted cement was clear except for the potted evergreens shaped into piercing spirals that reached towards the ceiling.

"What're you looking for?"

"Nothing."

"Hmm," Reagan said, twisting her key into the deadbolt and pushing open the massive door. The light from the porch cast the interior in shadow, with only a sliver of light that crossed the floor and reflected off the shiny marble tiles. Chad noted the silence. No TV, no barking dog, it was eerily quiet even for Chad, who craved solitude.

"He's probably in his study," Reagan walked down the entryway and to the right.

"Of course he is, aren't they always in the study in the movies of the rich and famous?" Chad whispered with a hint of sarcasm.

"Dad?"

Looking around behind Reagan, Chad didn't see anything. It was too dark. "Is there a light switch?"

"No he's got a lamp on the credenza by the wall."

"Great, what's a credenza, and what wall?"

"Here, silly."

The muted colors of the room seemed to drink in and absorb the soft light, making Chad squint to see. *I must be getting old. I can't see shit in here,* she thought, taking in the ornate décor.

"He's not in here. Maybe he's in the TV room?"

Chad followed Reagan on her wild goose chase through the lower levels of the massive structure. Grabbing her arm, she swung Reagan around and looked at her. "He said he was sick, maybe he's at the hospital. Why don't you call him before we send out the bloodhounds?"

"I can't, I left my phone in the car."

She rolled her eyes and handed her cell phone to Reagan. "Use mine. What's the closest hospital from here? I'll start there. We'll check on him and then get you home. I'm tired and I'm getting crankier by the minute."

"So I see," Reagan said, snatching the phone out

of Chad's hand.

As Reagan punched the numbers into her phone, Chad couldn't help but scan the hallway around them. Huge oil pictures hung on the wall. One of a little girl holding a puppy made Chad smile.

"Oh, that's me when I was eight. Daddy thought it would make for a wonderful painting."

Chad laughed as Reagan slipped on the daddy reference. She was still daddy's little girl, regardless of how old she was. "Of course it is."

Chad heard a faint ringing upstairs and cocked her head to listen. Following the sound, she started to climb the stairs towards the noise.

"Where are you going?"

"Upstairs, I think that's your father's phone you're calling."

"Wait. What?"

"Don't hang up. Let the phone ring so I can find him."

"Wait, Chad. Wait."

Chad sprinted up the stairs. At a minimum, Frank should have heard them come in. He definitely would have reacted when Reagan was calling to him in the study, and now she was worried. Pulling herself along with the handrail, she took the stairs three at a time. Hitting the landing at the top, she stopped and listened again for the ringing. It was coming from her right. She walked towards a door that was partly open.

"Is his bedroom this way?"

"Yes," Reagan said, still halfway down the stairs.

She pushed the door open and fumbled for a light switch. "Shit, credenza, right?" She practically knocked over a small table that held a lamp. "Don't you people believe in central wiring? Fuck." Twisting the knob on the lamp, she saw a man lying face down on the floor by the bed.

She shouted to Reagan who was just making the top of the stairs, "Call 9-1-1!"

"Why, what's happened?"

"I don't know. Call 911, now!" She knelt next to Frank.

Slowly she turned him over and felt his neck for a pulse. Weak, she thought. "Frank?"

Reagan burst through the doorway yelling, "Daddy!"

Chad felt his face and then his hands. His skin was cold and clammy. Picking up his hand, she looked at his fingernails and noticed a bluish tint to the nail bed. Considering the past days only one thought came to mind when Chad saw this, poisoning. Chad shook Frank, hoping for a response. His body was struggling to take in enough oxygen, which meant his breathing was compromised. Pushing his mouth open, she pulled on his chin and positioned his airway so she could start rescue breathing.

"Daddy, can you hear me?" Reagan pushed Chad out of the way and cupped his face, tears streaming down her cheeks. "Daddy...please...say something."

Reagan's desperate tone pulled at Chad, but she had to stay focused. "Reagan, EMS will be here any minute. Let me try to help him breathe and then we can get him downstairs, so that when they get here we're ready."

"No, you might hurt him."

"I won't hurt him, now move and let me do my job."

"Reagan," Frank's voice was barely a whisper as he tried to speak. "Honey, you're home. I told you not to come over. I'm fine really." His cold hand rested on Reagan's arm as he tried to get up.

"Frank, don't try and get up. We've got an ambulance on the way." Chad turned to Reagan and shook her. "Reagan, grab a blanket and let's cover your father. He's cold and I'm afraid he might be going into shock."

"Shock. What do you mean shock?"

"Grab a blanket and then hit number one on my phone. It will dial Marcus. Tell him to meet us at the hospital. Now. Do it," Chad ordered as she tucked the blanket around Frank.

Chad hated being so forceful with Reagan but she was already freaking out over her father. If their roles were reversed, Chad probably would be, too, but someone had to be in control and control was what she was good at.

"Frank, can you tell me what happened?"

"Chad, what a relief you're here with Reagan. Don't let anything happen to my little girl. She doesn't have anyone to watch out for her when I'm gone."

"You're not going anywhere, Frank. Now, can you tell me what happened?"

"I don't know. I was feeling a little sick, so I ate some soup, took a shower, and was going to bed. The next thing I know was this..." he said, weakly moving his fragile hand down his body.

"Okay. How long have you been feeling sick?"

"Oh, maybe—" His eyes stared off into space and then he refocused on Chad. "Watch out for my little girl, please."

"Frank, you're going to be fine. Just stay with me

here." Chad cupped his hand between hers and started rubbing it.

The sound of sirens drawing closer pierced the silence.

Chapter Twenty-five

Reagan looked down at her father. A tube sticking out of his mouth was connected to a giant ball that a paramedic was squeezing. His chest rising and falling with each squeeze as the paramedic did his job. A death grip was the only thing keeping Reagan connected to her father, and she refused to let go, fearing if she did she would lose him forever. The sounds of the ambulance, the siren, and the working equipment filled the small space, but didn't compete with the laser focus she had on her father. He would make it. He had to make it, she needed him to make it. She had pleaded, begged and prayed to whatever God would listen to her in the short ride to the hospital. She begged for his life, bargained with her own if he would be spared, and still she felt hopeless watching his gray motionless face.

Seconds felt like hours before the ride finally ended at the door of the emergency room. When the doors swished open, the paramedics unloaded him and briefed the doctors on his vital signs.

"Miss, you'll need to move. Miss?"

"What, of course. I'm sorry," Reagan said looking around at all the activity around her father. *Chad. Where was Chad?* she thought as she felt her father's hand slip from hers. Her world seemed to tunnel in on her as she watched him move farther down the hall. Farther away from her, further from life.

"Reagan." She heard Chad's voice but couldn't move. She was rooted in place, afraid that if she moved, she would crumble to the wet ground. She felt herself turned and wrapped in warm arms. "Don't worry, it'll be okay."

She could barely move her arms to wipe the tears from her eyes. Trapped, she felt trapped by circumstances, by Chad's embrace, by the thoughts that her father might die. As she wrestled with her emotions, she felt Chad's arms tighten around her. They were warm and protective, yet smothering.

"Let me go."

"Reagan, relax, he's with the doctors. They'll do everything they can. Come on, let's go inside and see what we can find out."

"He can't die, Chad. He just can't die and leave me here all alone. I won't let him."

"I know. I know. They're going to do everything they can. Come on, let's go inside and sit down."

Reagan let herself be led like a child into the waiting room and placed in a chair. Pulling the sleeve to her sweater, she wiped her eyes, already rough from crying.

"Let me get you some tissues."

Reagan pulled her legs up and tucked herself in a tight ball. She couldn't wipe at the tears fast enough as they streamed down her face. Her body heaved and shuddered each time she took a breath and released it. *What would she do if something happened to her father?* she wondered. Resting her forehead on her knees, she sobbed. She couldn't imagine being alone, all alone to fend for herself. She had always anticipated taking over the company, but not without some fatherly advice every now and then. As her chest heaved, her heart felt as if someone had just shoved a knife through it, and the pain was agonizing, the despair wrenching.

"Reagan? Reagan, look at me." She couldn't. She just couldn't raise her head to acknowledge Chad in anyway. A warm whisper in her ear made her lean into the soothing voice. "I know you think you can't be strong, but you must, for your father."

Strong, safe arms wrapped around her again and she melted against Chad's body. If she could suck strength from Chad she would, but it didn't work that way. She would have to dig down and find it, if she could, just not right now.

☙ ☙ ❧ ❧

Watching Reagan sit in the fetal position in the chair had almost done Chad in. She could almost feel the pain wracking Reagan's body with each sob. Chad felt Reagan mold against her, as she leaned her head on Chad's shoulder. Brushing her cheek against the soft hair under it, Chad tried to whisper words of encouragement, but it didn't seem to have any affect. Reagan only sobbed harder with each wordy caress.

"Ms. Reynolds," a doctor said, walking into the waiting room.

Reagan practically jumped out of Chad's arms as she meet the doctor halfway.

"Yes, I'm Reagan Reynolds. What's wrong with my father?"

"Well to be honest, we don't know yet. We're running tests and hopefully, we'll know something soon. We've stabilized him, but right now, he's on life support. Does he have a medical directive?"

"A medical directive?"

"Instructions in case he's unable to make decisions for himself," Chad said, rubbing her hand across Reagan's back for support. She knew this was going to be tough for Reagan, so she steeled herself for the imminent collapse she knew was coming. "In a nutshell it lets the doctors know who should make decisions for him or it lets the doctors know if he wants to be taken off life support. But only if it looks like there is no hope."

"What? No! No, I'm his only family. I want him to stay. You do whatever you need to do to save him. Money is no object here."

"Right now he's stable, but you should be prepared for any outcome. At his age—"

"Stop. You go back there and you fix him. You do whatever it takes. Do you understand me?"

Reagan's authoritative tone didn't surprise Chad, but she knew that as soon as the doctor left she would puddle into a weeping heap.

"Can I speak to you," the doctor said to Chad.

"Of course." Chad sat Reagan down and knelt at eye level. "Let me see what I can do, okay?"

"Thanks."

"No problem."

Chad let the doctor guide her down the hall so they could talk. "Are you two involved?"

"You could say that."

"Well without divulging patient information, I would recommend that you prepare Ms. Reynolds for the possibility that her father may not make it. The prognosis is not good and I don't want to see the hospital in a protracted legal battle." Tossing up his hands, he continued, "I'm not saying she's going to sue, but it's clear that she's very emotional right now and we really are doing our best."

"I understand." Chad looked back at Reagan, who was staring at them. "It's just a hunch, but I think you should check for poison?"

"Poison?"

"The family's been having some death threats and we've had one incident already."

"Have you called the police?"

"We have someone a little higher than that looking into this, but yes the authorities have been called."

The doctor sighed and then admitted, "Let's do a blood draw and see what we can find. We have a protocol for drug overdoses and poisoning, so I'll start there and see if we can get some better results with Mr. Reynolds."

"Thanks."

"You still should prepare Ms. Reynolds, just in case."

"Understood."

"I'll let you know if I find anything."

"What did he say?"

Chad rocked on her heels, as she hands stuffed in her pockets. Chad wondered if she should let Reagan in on her suspicions or if she should wait. She hoped she was wrong, but as she put more pieces of the puzzle in place, she saw only one logical explanation for everything. Still, she would wait until she was sure.

"Well?"

"He's just worried about you. He said I should keep an eye on you since this is a difficult time," Chad lied.

"I'm calling bullshit on that. So what did he

really say?"

"I told you. He's worried."

"Can I see my dad?"

"I'll check."

The visit with Frank was quick and emotional. Reagan practically threw herself across his bed, sobbing uncontrollably. It was all Chad could do to get her out of the room, with a promise to return later that morning. Chad found Marcus waiting for her in the waiting room.

"News?"

"Not yet."

"Okay, I need you to do me a favor. Go back to the house and find anything that Frank might have been eating or drinking in the last few days. Bring in everything that's been opened. Look through the trash in the house and in the trashcan and bring in everything. Take it to the lab. I called ahead and they're waiting for you. Have them test everything for poisons—rat poison, Ricin, anything and everything. I need this as soon as possible."

"You think he's been poisoned?"

"I don't think Reagan was ever the target. I think it's been Frank this whole time and whoever did this needed Reagan out of the way."

"Shit. She played right into their hands. They knew she wouldn't take the death threat seriously."

"Yep, they knew she'd leave town to prove a point and take any security with her. Maybe it began as a game. Maybe this was their plan all along. I don't know, but we're going to find out."

"Have you said anything to Reagan, yet?"

"Not until I have some proof. So, let's get that proof and hope we can save Frank's life."

Chapter Twenty-six

Time dragged for Reagan as she sat watching her father sleep. Once again, her death grip on his hand was the only thing keeping her connected to her father. Monitors beeped around her, the swoosh of the machine that kept him breathing barely registered with her. Resting her head against his hand she hoped—no wished—she could transfer her life energy into him. She rubbed his hand against her cheek; glad it was warm again. If she hadn't left, none of this would have happened, she told herself. She often chided him on his long hours, his bad eating habits, and careless disregard for his health. Now he was in the hospital, sick.

"Dad, you've got to get well. We've got lots to do," she whispered, wiping at tears that had started to fall again. "I need you, Daddy."

Reagan wasn't ready to look at life without the last of her family. She adored her father, and did her best to emulate his best qualities. She wasn't quite sure she had succeeded, but she promised herself if he survived, she would do whatever it took to be the kind of leader her father was.

"Reagan, we should go. You need your rest and you aren't doing Frank any good pushing yourself like this. Someone has to be present at the company in the morning and you're it,"

Reagan felt Chad's strong hands massage her

shoulders in comfort. Chad was right, someone needed to step up and take the reins. The company has to see strong leadership, not someone caving under the adversity.

"You're right. I should to be ready for tomorrow. Please tell me you know what's happening here." Reagan hoped that someone had answers for whatever was going on.

"I would just be guessing, Reagan, but I think we need to talk."

"What's going on, Chad?"

"We'll talk outside. I don't want to discuss this now." Chad nodded her head towards Frank.

"Goodbye, Daddy," Reagan whispered. She leaned down and kissed her father's cheek. "I'll be back in a couple of hours."

She let herself be pulled against Chad's lean frame as they walked out of the hospital. She was tired, empty, and overwhelmed. Regardless, she had to step up and put on a strong face for the sake of the company. Reagan wasn't sure she could do it alone in her present state. She needed help. Marcy.

"I'll call Marcy. She can pull together the administrator and board for a meeting. I want to get an idea of where everything stands, and she can probably do that quickly."

"No, I—I—uhm, I don't think that's a good idea."

"Excuse me?"

"Let's get in the car and we'll talk." Chad opened the door to the SUV and ushered her in. "Rita, can you take us to the coffee house? I think I need a pick me up."

"I have coffee at my house."

"I know, but I want privacy."

"In a coffee house?"

"Out in the open where I can watch who comes and goes and where I know there won't be any listening devices. We haven't been back to sweep your house, so humor me."

"I don't understand. You think it's someone I know? Who, Marcy? No, I won't believe it's her."

"Exactly, it gives me the perspective to be objective. I'm not colored by a relationship. I can see things for what they really are, not what I want them to be."

"You mean like us." Reagan knew her words would poke at Chad.

"I don't follow."

"Well, you ran away from me, from us, from the possibilities." Reagan locked eyes with Chad, defying her to deny it.

"This conversation isn't about what's happened in the past few days. We're talking about your father's life."

"Okay, then talk," Reagan ordered.

She watched Chad shuffle the sugar packets between her fingers like a magician weaving a coin back and forth over her knuckles. If anxiety were a drug, Reagan was ready to overdose. Snatching the weaving packets, she tossed them on the table and pushed out a sigh.

"What is going on?"

"First, just let me say that I wanted to talk to your father about this and let him be the one to tell you."

The buzzing in the room was starting to get to Reagan. She had been patient with Chad for over an hour, but her patience was not only wearing thin, she was wearing it out. It hadn't just been a week of ups and downs, she had been on a non-stop roller coaster that had lost its brakes, and was racing into a turn at breakneck speed, ready to career off the tracks. Her head was throbbing. She felt a migraine was just around the corner. Her body begged for sleep, a hot bath, or a throbbing orgasm—any would cleanse her system, she was sure.

"Come on, Chad. I need to get back to the hospital and be with my father. That can't happen until I've had an hour of sleep, called a meeting of the board, and talked to upper management. I have to disseminate the factual information about my father."

Reagan's head lolled forward. She was almost too tired to sit up. Chad's warm hands grasped hers and held them tight. "Reagan, I don't think you were ever the target."

"What?"

"I think whoever is behind all of this wanted you out of the way and they played you, your father, and me. They knew you would want to go and meet each board member personally, thus getting you out of the way. I think your father was the target all along and then they would focus on you later."

"They? They who?" Reagan scrubbed her face. She couldn't believe what she was hearing. "No one made me go, I went on my own."

"Who did you talk to about your plans?"

"My dad."

"Anyone else?"

Reagan shook her head. She wasn't someone who had to tell everyone every detail of her life. She didn't need to build herself up and boast about what she was doing or going to do.

"No one?"

"No, who would I tell?"

"Marcy? Did you talk to Marcy about going?"

"Well yeah, but—oh no, you don't know Marcy like I do." Reagan shook her head and stood. "No way, no way, Chad. I'm telling you that there's no way she's involved."

"Did you talk with her about your plans?"

"Yeah, briefly, but she was completely supportive. She thought it was a good idea. In fact, she helped me get all the board members info together so I would know everything about them. Hell, she even helped me find out their weaknesses, their hobbies and—this is too much, no way. Marcy's been with the company forever. She's been a trusted employee for, shit, ten years at least."

"Huh," Chad said, walking Reagan out of the coffee shop.

After all the drama Reagan had been through in the past week, this was the last straw and Chad was going to find out just how out-of-line she was. Things between her and Marcy were fine. Marcy had handled the break-up fine. In fact, she had made it seem like it was all her idea, at first. But something about the way Marcy acted after that didn't set well with her. Work had taken suddenly taken over Marcy, she was never late, she stayed behind after everyone was gone, and worked weekends when no one else would volunteer. She suddenly had a sick feeling in the pit of her stomach and doubt ate at her. Was it Marcy? Why could someone so close to her and her father suddenly want to hurt them? What had they done to her? Her throat clenched as she felt her stomach cramp, sending bile up.

"I think I'm going to be sick." she said, grabbing for Chad.

Doubling over, she heaved the coffee she had just consumed. The sickening feeling didn't ease, it only intensified as she remembered the nights she had spent entwined in Marcy's arms, now the embrace of an attempted killer. She felt her hair pulled away from her face as she doubled over again, gagging on what was left of the contents of her stomach.

"You okay?" Chad rubbed small circles on Reagan's back.

Reagan shook her head. "If anything happens to my father, I would never forgive myself. It's all my fault my father was in a coma and might die." Wiping at the tears she finally stood, clutching her stomach.

"Look, this isn't your fault so don't even go there." Chad cupped Reagan's face, wiping tears away. "We don't know if it's her, but trust me, I'm going to find out. Okay?"

"I'm going to call her right now." Reagan pulled her cell phone and flicked it open. She would get to the bottom of what was going on if it killed her. Before she could punch the buttons that would bring her answers, Chad grabbed her cell phone. "Hey, give that back."

"No. You're not going to do anything rash. Besides, I want to catch her red-handed and I can't do that if you give her a heads-up that we're suspicious of her."

Reagan held her hand out for her cell phone, but Chad shook her head and tucked it in her blazer.

"I still can't believe Marcy could have played me like that. I mean, we were so close. She was...."

Chad pulled her close and tight. Burying her head on Chad's chest, she tried to let go of the last vestiges of shame but couldn't seem to relinquish her hold on it. She knew it would stay with her for a long time if her father survived. It was her fault, all her fault.

᪥᪥᪥᪥

Quietly, they rode side-by-side, neither wanting to say the wrong thing. Staring at her hands, Chad laced her fingers together and then unlaced them. Nervous energy raced through her body, her mind bounced around ideas trying to think about ways to catch Marcy. She was sure Reagan was thinking the same thing; only she was envisioning ways to make Marcy pay for what she'd done to her father.

Chad studied Reagan's stoic face. Her soft features were in direct contrast to Chad's own boyish looks.

"Will you stay? I mean—I don't want to be alone." Reagan paused, looking out at the dark night, her face barely reflected back from the tinted glass. Chad knew she should probably say no, but it was clear everything she had just told Reagan had left her reeling. She could barely wrap her mind around the fact that Marcy might have a kid, let alone the possibility it was Reagan's brother. However, now she had to consider the fact that Marcy might be the one trying to kill the Reynolds's. Maybe not Reagan, but her father.

"Sure, I've got my kit in the car so I'm good for the morning."

"Kit?"

"Oh sorry, my overnight kit."

"Hmm." Reagan flashed Chad a faint smile before going back to studying something far away in the deepest of darkest nights. "I guess I should apologize for my behavior."

Chad cocked her head towards Reagan, whose pained tone was evident. "No need." Chad patted Reagan's folded hands, covering them with her own.

"I guess I should admit you were right. Someone was trying to kill us, well at least my father."

"Reagan—"

Still not looking at Chad, Reagan gently threw up a hand to stop her from continuing. "I know when to admit I was wrong, Chad. I was wrong. Almost dead wrong, in fact."

Reagan's shoulders sagged at the weight of the revelation. Her pain sat out for everyone to see, defeat written all over her face. Chad slid over to wrap her arm around Reagan's shoulders and pull her close. She had wanted to prove Reagan was wrong the whole time, to show the brash, arrogant woman that she wasn't *a piece of meat* hanging around her neck, waiting for a chance to strangle her. The winning seemed insignificant now. Chad's body shook with small tremors as Reagan started to cry. She lifted Reagan's chin to gaze into tear-filled eyes.

"Why are you crying?"

"My father counted on me and I let him down. I—I—I missed it. I had no idea that Marcy would do something so—"

"Ruthless?"

"Exactly. I trusted her, Chad. She knew everything about me, my personal life, who I dated. She has the keys to my house and my father's house. I trusted her." Devastation flashed across Reagan's face as she cried harder against Chad's blazer.

"Look, we don't know for sure it's her, but don't worry. If it is her, she won't get away with this, I promise."

There was no way Chad would tell Reagan about the possibility that Frank had fathered another child with Marcy. She was even more determined that Frank would live, if only to be the one to break the news to Reagan. After Chad broke it to him first, of course. The problem with secrets was they never stayed hidden for long and when they came out, it was usually devastating.

Reagan relaxed in Chad's embrace. Long, deep breaths replaced the small tremors and Chad knew Reagan had finally fallen asleep. In about twenty minutes they would be at Reagan's house and then she could finally get some rest, too.

"Sophia?" Chad whispered.

"Hmm?"

"Call someone and get them over to Reagan's house. It seems Marcy has a set of keys to both her house and Frank's. I want them to sweep the place, pull the tubes of toothpaste, open beverages, and food containers in the frig need to be tossed. In fact, tell them anything that's been opened that could be compromised should be pulled aside and tested for poison."

If Frank had innocently ingested poison in the soup or something else Marcy had given him, there was no doubt she could do the same thing with Reagan. It would look like Reagan had caught whatever bug Frank had when she visited him, all very innocent if the doctors hadn't tested Frank for poison. Who would suspect it anyway? Chad felt her body relax just a little. She had been playing defense to Marcy's offense and now that she was on to her, Chad could bait the trap easily. Reagan would be the bait.

"Chad, Marcus said he and the team would be at Reagan's when we get there. They just dropped off the stuff from Frank's place at the lab. He said to tell you that he would have results in the morning."

"Good. Tell him I'm staying with Reagan just in case Marcy shows up. I've got a plan to catch that little bitch."

Chapter Twenty-seven

Gently laying Reagan on the bed, Chad considered her predicament. She could leave her fully dressed and cover her with a blanket. Or she could undress her, cover her with a blanket, and go down the hall to sleep in a spare bedroom. As she weighed her options, she reached out and slid her hand down Reagan's ankle cupping the heel as she pulled Reagan's stilettos off, then dropping them to the floor. The slight thud, barely registered with Reagan. Chad held her foot and let her gaze lazily make its way up the curve of Reagan's leg. Reagan's dress had worked its way up to her ass when she was placed on the bed and now Chad could only ogle the shapely limbs, remembering the last time they were wrapped around her hips. Blushing, Chad looked around for a blanket so she could cover Reagan's sexy body, chastising herself for thinking of Reagan sexually at a time like this. Pulling a blanket from the same huge closet she had locked Reagan in a week earlier, she tried to lay it on her gently, but ended up covering her face as she flicked it out to unfurl it.

"Damn," she whispered, pulling it down just enough so Reagan could breathe.

Turning to leave, she heard a soft voice whisper from behind her, "You aren't going to leave me dressed are you?"

"No, *you're* going to leave you dressed." Chad

looked over, barely able to see Reagan's eyes watching her. Reagan stretched, and her legs and arms slipped out from under the blanket. "You said you were going to stay."

"I am, I'm going to go take a shower and sleep in the guest room down the hall. I'll be close."

Reagan swung her legs over the side of the bed and stretched her toes, before getting up. "Could you unzip me?"

Chad waivered. She had done this before, when Reagan caught her naked from the waist up and it had almost led to sex. Her hands shook as she grasped the zipper pull with one hand and the top of the dress with the other.

Zzzrrrrppppp.

In the next moment, Reagan had shimmied out of the dress, and Chad's eyes followed its path down Reagan's legs and on to the floor. Without another word between the two women, Chad practically ran down the hall and shut the door to the guest room. Unprofessional? Maybe. Safer this way, yes.

Chad pushed aside the kit with her clothes that Sophia had placed on the bed. Flouncing on the mattress, she threw her arms wide and kicked off her loafers. She could fall asleep right here and now if it wasn't for the fact that she desperately needed a shower. Two round trips in one day and her jet lag left her feeling as if she had three too many shots of cold Tres Generations tequila. The bed spun, her eyes rolled back in her head and she grabbed the comforter, trying to stop it all.

"You okay?"

Chad bolted upright at the sound of Reagan's voice, the spinning nearly knocking her to the floor from a sitting position. Closing her eyes, she grabbed her knees and took a deep breath. Exhaustion, she felt it from the tips of her toes to her head that was circling, trying to land safely on the pillow.

"Yeah, I'm good. I just need to get a quick shower and then hit the pillow."

"Hmm."

"You okay?" Chad asked, finally looking up at Reagan. She wore a robe and a towel wound around her head. *How had she taken a shower so fast?* Chad wondered.

She chuckled a little too loudly. Reagan gave her a cross look.

"What's so funny?"

"Nothing. I just haven't seen someone wear a towel like that in a long time."

"No, I don't suppose with your short hair you need to worry about wet hair down your back," Reagan said. She put her hands on her hips, trying to take back control of the situation. "But I have seen the way you wear a towel and it's kinda—"

"Stop. We are not going there tonight." Chad stood to pull control back in her court.

"I was just saying."

"I know what you were saying, but not this time. Besides, aren't you tired? I feel like I've been run over by a Mack truck." Chad tossed her blazer on the chair and started the process of taking her gear off, while trying to ignore Reagan and the freshly scrubbed scent that swirled around her. Reagan reached around and helped unbutton Chad's pants and began to pull them down. Chad grabbed Reagan's hands to stop their progress and turned around to face her.

That was the wrong thing to do. Reagan's hooded

eyes spoke volumes as they lingered on Chad's lips. Suddenly uncomfortable, Chad tried to step back, but Reagan's hands slid behind her back and held their hips tightly together. Reagan's warm hands glided up her back to pull her closer. Their breasts practically touching sent a small shimmer through Chad. It wouldn't take much to stoke the smoldering fire within her. As Reagan pushed up on her toes, she felt the robe give way and her smooth body pushing and sliding against Chad. She grasped Reagan's shoulders and held her firmly.

"We shouldn't be doing this, Reagan," she said, even as Reagan's wet lips found her neck and began a slow, deliberate caress.

Chad's body amped up, nipples peaked, her hips pressed for more contact with Reagan. Her fingers gently bit into Reagan's shoulders. One hand slid down the curve of Reagan's breast, reaching around and grabbing her ass. Chad found herself starting to grind softly against Reagan. Instinctively, she grabbed Reagan's ass with both hands and lifted her up. Reagan responded, wrapping her legs around Chad's hips as Chad seductively pulled her open from underneath. She could feel the wetness as her fingertips grasped Reagan upper thighs to hold her tight. Reagan's scent wafted up between them, and like catnip to a kitty, it sent Chad into a frenzy.

Chad's lips glided along Reagan's neck briefly before finding her open mouth. Without hesitation, she took control and devoured Reagan's kisses. Heat coursed around them as they worked Chad's clothes off. Buttons flew when Reagan pulled at the front, shoving the shirt down Chad's arms, and holding her captive. Chad could feel the slickness of Reagan on her stomach as she continued to grind against her abs, sending her deeper into the sexual abyss.

"Down," Chad commanded, releasing Reagan's legs.

Sliding to her knees, she buried her nose in the small patch of hair above Reagan's clit. Pulling her hips closer, Chad took a deep breath and slipped her tongue between the folds. She felt Reagan's hand pushing her head, further consent to continue her exploration. Flattening her tongue, she rubbed it against the distended clit, pushing the hood back and flicking it. Chad's body stiffened when she heard Reagan moan and press her head harder against her pussy.

"Chad?" Sophia's voice came through the door, followed by a knock.

Jerking back, she tried to center herself, but the smell of Reagan on her lips was making it hard to focus.

"Yeah."

"I think we have a situation."

"What kind of situation?" Chad knew she should get off her knees and answer the door, but she hesitated in hopes that it was something minor Sophia could handle.

"A guest. I think you might want to see this before I alert Ms. Reynolds. It's Marcy Decker."

Chad looked up at Reagan, who had lost that lustful look. Her sober expression echoed her own feelings, but it seemed like there was something more behind the look. Standing, Reagan tied off her robe and started for the door. Grabbing her sleeve, Chad stopped Reagan and turned her around. "Stop, I don't want you going down there and confronting her. Let's see what she says. Besides, you're in my room dressed this way and I smell like—"

"Sex."

"I'll be right down, Sophia," Chad called. "Keep an eye on our visitor and make sure she doesn't touch anything. I'll go get Ms. Reynolds and bring her down."

"You got it."

Still holding onto Reagan's robe, Chad wondered if she might be helpful in setting a plan in motion.

"I need you to be calm and cool with Marcy. We've got to do this right, otherwise she could get off scot-free."

Reagan left to change, while Chad washed her face and changed into fresh clothes. Would tonight ever end? She pulled out her camera pen and switched it on, then clipped it to her pocket, and added a notepad. No one would suspect that Chad had video and audio surveillance at her fingertips, and if she was lucky she would catch Marcy red-handed.

She knocked on Reagan's door and waited. When she heard nothing, she pushed the door slightly and peaked around it. "Reagan?" She spotted Reagan sitting on the edge of the bed. She wasn't the hot, sexy woman who Chad had just tasted. Now she was crying with her head buried in her hands.

"Hey," Chad stroked Reagan's hair and bent down. "What's wrong?"

"What do you mean what's wrong? The person who tried to kill my father is down there, while I was up here trying to seduce you, and my father is lying in a hospital room dying. I am so fucked up."

"Hey, calm down. Let's deal with what we can and leave the rest in someone else's hands." Chad continued to stroke the soft locks of hair that cascaded down Reagan's back. Pulling her up, Chad pushed a few strands back and looked at Reagan. "If you can't face Marcy, then I'll just go down and tell her you're not seeing anyone."

"No, no. I've got this. I'm not going to let that little bitch get away with this. I'll kill her if I have to."

Great, now Reagan was on an emotional rollercoaster that Chad had to control, or the whole case could be blown out of the water. One minute Reagan was all business, the next a seductress, and finally she was a maniac killer—all within the span of twenty minutes. It had been a long time since Chad had to deal with the severe mood swings of a woman, and she wasn't sure she was ready for it right now.

"Calm down. Take a deep breath," Chad said, grabbing Reagan's shoulders. The look Reagan gave her almost made her laugh, but they had serious business to take care of so she pushed it down. Finally, Reagan took a deep breath and forced it out through pursed lips.

"Ready?" Reagan took another and pushed it out with a sigh.

"Calm, just remain calm."

Chapter Twenty-eight

Marcy sat in the study, calmly perusing a magazine. When Reagan entered, she jumped up and ran towards her. Throwing her arms around Reagan, she started to cry. What bullshit, she thought, half-heartedly returning the hug.

"Oh my god. I can't believe it's true, Reagan. Your father's in a coma. This is awful, truly awful." Marcy dabbed at phantom tears, while Reagan held her own just under the surface. "Are you all right? What can I do to help?"

"I'm fine, Marcy. Thank you for asking." It hurt to say the stilted words, but she didn't want to let on that she knew anything. "I understand that you were looking after my father. Thanks for doing that," Reagan said, taking both of Marcy's hands to lead her to the couch. She could feel Chad right on her heels as they sat down.

"Of course. You know I would do anything for you, Reagan." Marcy's smile made Reagan want to puke. How could she have been so wrong about Marcy? She had been intimate with this woman, Marcy knew things about her only a few women knew, and yet, she could be responsible for all the death threats, her father getting sick, everything. On the other hand, it just didn't seem possible. She knew Marcy.

Patting Marcy's hand reassuringly, she said, "I appreciate that, Marcy. How was my father the last time you saw him?"

"Fine. I mean he was a little under the weather, but other than that, he was his usual self. Laughing, joking, and talking about the upcoming board meeting." Marcy raised her hand to her open mouth. "Oh god, we'll need to cancel the board meeting."

Reagan narrowed her eyes. If Marcy were behind this, she would want the board meeting to go through, wouldn't she? If the board met now, Reagan was the logical choice to take over as interim president and that would fit into Marcy's plans. Something wasn't adding up.

Reagan quirked an eyebrow at Chad. Something stunk in this room and she suspected she was the only one without answers. Before she could say anything, Chad stepped forward, pulling a chair with her and sitting down in front of them.

"Ms. Decker, do you mind if I ask you some questions?"

"No of course. What's this about?" Marcy looked from Chad to Reagan, who shrugged her shoulders. She didn't have a clue where Chad was going with this, but she had been told to play along so she would, for now.

"Well, first let me say thank you for keeping an eye on Frank. He was lucky to have you there to watch out for him."

"Of course, I would do anything for Frank," she said, looking over at Reagan and patting her hand. "And for Ms. Reynolds."

Reagan returned the smile half-heartedly and squeezed Marcy's hands. Reagan wasn't sure where Chad was going with this. If it were up to her she would come right out directly with her questions. She could only sit back and let Chad do her job, especially since, in the past, she had done everything she could to prevent that.

"When did you notice Frank starting to get sick?

"Oh gosh, He just—really started getting sick—hmm, let me think," she put her finger to her lip and tapped it. "I guess soon after Ms. Reynolds left. I figured it was the stress getting to him and he would bounce back, the way he always does."

"Does he get sick like this often?"

"Oh no, Frank's—I mean Mr. Reynolds—is as healthy as a horse. Wouldn't you say Ms. Reynolds?"

Reagan studied Marcy, intent on trying to catch her in a lie. Her face looked as it always did, soft and serene. In fact, she had never seen Marcy stressed, which was what made her such an asset. Reagan felt disgust as she watched the woman she thought she'd known. Sophia entered the room with a tray of glasses. She set them on the coffee table and then whispered something in Chad's ear. Chad nodded and whispered something back, none of which Reagan could hear. It didn't matter because she doubted she could process any more information right now. Her single focus was getting answers to the list of questions that had begun to pile up in her head.

"When did you start seeing Mr. Reynolds?" Chad asked Marcy.

"What?"

"Let me repeat the question, when did you start seeing Mr. Reynolds?"

"You slept with my dad?"

"Ms. Morgan didn't ask me if I was sleeping with your father," Marcy told Reagan.

"Were you sleeping with Mr. Reynolds?" Chad

pressed.

Marcy shook her head and looked at the floor. Sitting straight up, she seemed to gather herself before she answered. "Your father's a very charming man and can be quite persuasive, Reagan."

"You slept with my dad." Reagan's monotone response belied the raging storm that was brewing inside her.

She gripped her hands tightly to still the tremor that began. She hoped to keep herself under control and not deck the woman sitting next to her.

"He's a grown adult, Reagan. He can do what he wants, when he wants, and with whom he wants."

Her smug response, accompanied by raised eyebrows suggested a dare of sorts that pricked a nerve in Reagan.

"So you do admit to sleeping with Mr. Reynolds?" Chad cut in between the two women.

"That was over a year ago, a brief fling and nothing more. Reagan, I'm sorry you had to find out about it this way, with your dad in the hospital and all. I had hoped you wouldn't find out. You're father promised me you wouldn't, but it seems that Ms. Morgan is persistent."

"That's it, a brief fling and nothing more? That's how you work, isn't it? First me and then my father? What were you doing, making the rounds to see if you could get a piece of the action?" Reagan's shrill voice pierced the air.

"Oh, Reagan, please. Aren't you being a tad over dramatic? I mean really? We had fun, but you said yourself that you weren't the marrying type. It was fun, and no one got hurt."

"And my father?"

Frustrated with the line of questioning, Chad was starting to lose her patience with the overly calm Marcy Decker.

"Ms. Decker, can I ask you a question?"

"Of course, but I thought you already were?"

Chad watched Marcy tense. They had been at this for over an hour, neither Reagan nor Chad had slept in the past twenty-four, and tension was definitely running high in the room. Chad turned her body towards Marcy, rested her elbows on her knees, and kept writing on her pad. She knew the digital pen was picking up everything the two were saying.

"Ms. Decker, you said earlier that you've been with the company for over ten years."

"Yes." she looked down counting on her fingers. "Yes, that's about right."

"When did you get pregnant with Frank Reynolds child?"

"What?" Two voices blurted out in unison. Chad looked from Marcy to Reagan and back to Marcy.

Chad lost her patience. "When did you start fucking Mr. Reynolds? Before or after your affair with Reagan?"

"What are you talking about, Chad?" Reagan broke into the questioning.

"Ms. Reynolds, I'm just trying to do my job. Perhaps you would like to step out and give Ms. Decker and I some privacy."

Chad looked at Marcy, still calm and serene, not the least bit unnerved by the accusation. Reagan, on the other hand, looked like someone just stolen her favorite doll.

"Can I see you outside, Ms. Morgan?"

"No. I'm sorry, if you don't like the line of questions, but I have a job to do, Ms. Reynolds."

"Ms. Morgan."

"Ms. Reynolds." The challenge had clearly been issued, but Chad wasn't biting. "Ms. Decker, when exactly did you start and stop fucking Mr. Reynolds?"

"What?"

"It takes nine months to have a child so—"

"I—I—uhm, I never had a child with Mr. Reynolds."

"What?"

Chad felt bad dropping such a bomb shell without preparing Reagan, but she had Marcy right where she wanted her. Chad hated to do it, but Frank's life was on the line and time was wasting with the too serene, too calm, Ms. Decker.

Marcy and Reagan both sat stunned at the accusation. Chad leaned back in her chair taking copious notes and stopping to point her pen at Marcy, who started to open her mouth and then just left it agape.

Reagan, on the other hand, appeared as though someone had just punched her in the stomach. Reagan clenched her middle as if she were going to be sick, little beads of sweat dotted her upper lip, and her face went pale. Shock, Chad knew it when she saw it.

"Sophia, can I have two glasses of water? Make sure it's tap water please."

"Yes, ma'am."

The silence hung in the room like a looming cloud of death, hovering just above their heads, waiting to drop its dangerous cargo any minute. Chad looked from one woman to the other, yet neither spoke. Reagan looked over in astonishment at Marcy and studied her.

"You had a child with my dad?"

"Are you going to believe this—this—"

Chad quirked an eyebrow when she locked her gaze on Marcy, daring her to continue. She'd had just about enough of Ms. Decker's crap and was ready to pop open the surprise gift she had waiting for her.

"Careful," Chad warned.

"Answer the question, Marcy. Did you have a child with my father?"

"We had sex, yes."

Reagan's gasp became a choking sound as she coughed from inhaling too quickly. Thumping her chest, she took the glass of water Chad handed her and took a quick sip. Grabbing the glass back before she dropped it, Chad gave Reagan a warning glare and then turned towards Marcy.

"That wasn't the question. Answer the fucking question, Marcy."

"I have no idea what you're talking about, Ms. Morgan."

Marcy's nonchalant shrug gave way to the typical eye-roll Chad recognized in people buying time to reconstruct the truth. Pressing further, she continued. "Ms. Decker, are you familiar with a young man named, Jason?"

As if in slow motion, Marcy's cool, calm demeanor went stone cold. Her eyes narrowed and focused like a laser on Chad, as if burrowing what would be the first of many small holes through her. Her jaw set tight as she ground her teeth in an almost animalistic reaction that faded as quickly as it had happened.

"I'm sorry, Jason who?"

Chad reached behind her for the folder Sophia held out and extracted a picture. She hadn't seen it yet, but as it passed from her hand to Marcy's, she could see the fleeting resemblance to Frank Reynolds. The soft brown eyes and square jaw were a dead giveaway to the young boy's parentage. Watching Reagan's expression for signs of recognition, she waited for the now sullen woman to say something when she saw the picture.

It was hard not to notice Reagan's reaction when she finally looked up from the picture. Her glance was accusatory and her eyes frozen. Reagan stiffened and then clenched her hands tightly in her lap. Chad new it was only a matter of time before she exploded, so she would have to be quick.

"I'm sure you recognize your son, Ms. Decker."

"I'm sure I don't know what you're taking about. This is my sister's son, Jake."

"You have a son? My father's son?"

"Are you going to take this woman's word over mine, Reagan? Seriously? We've known each other for a long time. When was I pregnant? Huh?" Marcy spit her venomous words at Reagan. "I've been with you and the company the whole time. It takes nine months to have a child. Don't you think I would have been showing if I was pregnant? I've gave my whole life for you and your father and this is how you treat me?" Marcy continued peppering Reagan with questions. "I've hardly taken a vacation, let alone take any personal time. I've given the company everything. I've lived and breathed Reynolds Holdings. Why would I hide something like a child?"

Marcy moved forward over Reagan as the women went nose-to-nose. I've taken more crap than a normal employee should, so why would I jeopardize my career?" Turning towards Chad she continued, "Who put you up to this?"

Chad didn't rattle easily. She sat forward on the edge of her chair, challenging Marcy. Chad caught movement out of the corner of her eye as Sophia moved to the edge of the couch.

"Bravo, Ms. Decker. Were you a thespian in college? I'm truly impressed with your range of emotion."

"You fucking bitch." Marcy's slap rang solid against Chad's cheek before Sophia could grab her.

"She's almost as deadly as you are Reagan. A little more wrist next time, Ms. Decker." Rubbing her cheek, Chad smiled and continued. "One more question, why did you poison Frank and Reagan, and did you do all of this on your own, or did you have help?" Chad fixed a laser stare on Reagan.

"What do you mean, poison me and my father?" Reagan said, visibly wincing at the accusation.

"Sophia just informed me that they found traces of arsenic in your food too, Reagan. Nice job of trying to throw all the suspicion on Marcy." Chad heard Reagan gasp but didn't look up from the notes she was taking. The accusation was hard enough, but the confirmation stung worse. "You were the only one who had the opportunity to put the cocaine in the flowers. The note on the car though, that was a nice touch. I guess my leaving gave you the time and opportunity to do it, didn't it?"

When she did finally look at Reagan, she was surprised to see a few tears streaming down her face. She wasn't sure what game Reagan was playing now, but the stunned look was a nice touch. Without saying a word, Reagan jumped on Marcy and started pummeling the unsuspecting woman.

"You fucking bitch, you tried to kill my father. I'm gonna kill you. That wasn't part of the plan." Reagan screamed, each strike landing firmly on Marcy's face. "I knew you couldn't be trusted and now I find out you've got a kid, too?"

Chad tried to pull Reagan off, but she was determined to follow through with her threat. Suddenly, Reagan had her hands around Marcy's throat and began choking her.

"Reagan, stop. You're only making matters worse for yourself. Stop before you do something you're going to regret." Chad wrapped her arms around Reagan and fell backwards against the couch.

"It's not how it looks Chad. I promise this wasn't what was supposed to happen," Reagan said, sobbing.

Sophia held Marcy's wrist behind her and stood her up, slapping cuffs on the belligerent woman.

"You stupid bitch. Shut your mouth before you say something you're going to regret," Marcy screamed.

"Fuck you. You were just supposed to make me the target, not my dad. I'm gonna kill you," Reagan said struggling to break free of Chad's grasp.

"You were always stupid like that Reagan. You think you're the smartest person in the room, now what are you going to do? What happens *if daddy dies*? You dumb, rich bitch." Marcy laughed as she was taken out of the room and outside.

Chapter Twenty-nine

Chad sat back in the uncomfortable chair, wishing she had better news for Frank, but it wasn't to be. She hadn't quite put all the pieces together until sitting in Reagan's house last night. She'd felt like a fool as she watched the interaction between the two women. Reagan had put a plan together with Marcy, which was her first mistake. Making herself the target was brilliant, if Chad did say so herself. All Reagan wanted was to prove to her father, she could handle any situation, no matter how dire. Reagan's second mistake was assuming Marcy wouldn't want more and try to eliminate Reagan, too. It was clear Reagan didn't know anything about the son Marcy had with Frank and Chad felt bad about springing that on Reagan, but it couldn't be avoided. Now she wished she hadn't played so loose and fast with the facts, Reagan looked genuinely shocked at the revelation. Marcy had lawyered up immediately and wasn't talking, but Reagan had money and resources, so she would get the best lawyer and probably walk sooner, rather than later.

Marcus confirmed Chad's suspicions when he told her that the prints found on the note left in the limo were Reagan's. The delivery of flowers to the hotel, Reagan's doing. The cocaine on the flowers was a slight of hand when Reagan smelled them. She had counted on Chad's domineering, take charge attitude to usher her away from Frank Reynolds, but it had let Marcy do her worst. While the plan was clever, it was too clean, too polished, and Marcy wasn't smart enough to pull it off alone. Money made people into monsters and Marcy was the worst kind of monster: cold and ruthless. Reagan on the other hand used her body as a commodity to be traded, a lure to suck in unsuspecting victims and then crush them. Board members, employees, ambassador's daughters, and anyone one else she felt was of value were the stock-in-trade, including Chad. If it could be manipulated like currency, Reagan traded in it. Chad was only sorry she found out too late in the game to protect what little of her heart she had shared.

Chad pulled out the picture of the little boy who looked exactly like his father. He was a pawn in all of this, too. Innocent, young and vulnerable, Jason Reynolds might inherit a fortune if Frank decided to disown his daughter. At a minimum, Frank would gain a son and keep his daughter; that was if he decided to forgive her for Marcy's deceit. Lucky for Frank, Chad's hunch had been right and the doctors were confident that they had caught the worst of it. If she had told Reagan her suspicions, Frank might be dead now. She was sure Reagan would have confronted Marcy before she had time to put all the pieces together. At which point Marcy could have done her worst to both Reagan and Frank; she had nothing to lose, if confronted with the truth.

Unfortunately, she had learned to trust no one, not even someone you slept with. Pulling her wallet out, she removed Dawn's picture and caressed it with her thumb. It was a gut punch every time she looked at it, but that was okay in Chad's book. It reminded her of better times, and right now, a stroll through the past was better than what the future held.

Looking over at a sleeping Frank, she wondered how she would tell him about Reagan. The good news was he had gained a son. Perhaps a son would make up for the deceit at the hands of his daughter. He could focus on his new heir-apparent, and maybe the raw edge of being deceived by his own flesh and blood wouldn't cut so deep, but she doubted it. Watching Reagan cuffed and put in the back of the police car had hurt more than she'd expected.

"Chad? Is that you?"

"Frank."

"Where's Reagan?"

"Frank, I'm afraid I've got...."

About the Author

Isabella lives in California with her wife and three sons. She teaches college, and speaks at high schools and universities on current issuses facing the LGBT community. She likes traveling with her wife, riding her motorcycle and spending time with her family.

She is a member of Gold Crown Literary Society, Romance Writers of America. She has written several short stories, and is now working on the follow-up to *American Yakuza - The Lies that Bind.*

You can follow her Facebook page or at the Sapphire Books website - www.sapphirebooks.com

Other Titles Available at Sapphire Books

Award winning novel - Always Faithful - By Isabella   ISBN - 978-0-9828608-0-9

Major Nichol "Nic" Caldwell is the only survivor of her helicopter crash in Iraq. She is left alone to wonder why she and she alone. Survivor's guilt has nothing on the young Major as she is forced to deal with the scars, both physical and mental, left from her ordeal overseas. Before the accident, she couldn't think of doing anything else in her life.

Claire Monroe is your average military wife, with a loving husband and a little girl. She is used to the time apart from her husband. In fact, it was one of the reasons she married him. Then, one day, her life is turned upside down when she gets a visit from the Marine Corps.

Can these two women come to terms with the past and finally find happiness, or will their shared sense of honor keep them apart?

GCLS Nominated - Scarlet Masquerade - By Jett Abbott ISBN - 978-0-9828608-1-6

What do you say to the woman you thought died over a century ago? Will time heal all wounds or does it just allow them to fester and grow? A.J. Locke has lived over two centuries and works like a demon, both figuratively and literally. As the owner of a successful pharmaceutical company that specializes in blood research, she has changed the way she can live her life. Wanting for nothing, she has smartly compartmentalized her life so that when she needs to, she can pick up and start all over again, which happens every twenty years or so.

Clarissa Graham is a university professor who has lived an obscure life teaching English literature. She has made it a point to stay off the radar and never become involved with anything that resembles her past life. She keeps her personal life separate from her professional one, and in doing so she is able to keep her secrets to herself. Suddenly, her life is turned upside down when someone tries to kill her. She finds herself in the middle of an assassination plot with no idea who wants her dead.

Broken Shield - By Isabella - ISBN - 978-0-9828608-2-3

Tyler Jackson, former paramedic now firefighter, has seen her share of death up close. The death of her wife caused Tyler to rethink her career choices, but the death of her mother two weeks later cemented her return to the ranks of firefighter. Her path of self-destruction and womanizing is just a front to hide the heartbreak and devastation she lives with every day. Tyler's given up on finding love and having the family she's always wanted. When tragedy strikes her life for a second time she finds something she thought she lost.

Ashley Henderson loves her job. Ignoring her mother's advice, she opts for a career in law enforcement. But, Ashley hides a secret that soon turns her life upside down. Shame, guilt and fear keep Ashley from venturing forward and finding the love she so desperately craves. Her life comes crashing down around her in one swift moment forcing her to come clean about her secrets and her life.

Can two women thrust together by one traumatic event survive and find love together, or will their past force them apart?

American Yakuza - By Isabella - ISBN - 978-0-9828608-3-0

Luce Potter straddles three cultures as she strives to live with the ideals of family, honor, and duty. When her grandfather passes the family business to her, Luce finds out that power, responsibility and justice come with a price. Is it a price she's willing to die for?

Brooke Erickson lives the fast-paced life of an investigative journalist living on the edge until it all comes crashing down around her one night in Europe. Stateside, Brooke learns to deal with a new reality when she goes to work at a financial magazine and finds out things aren't always as they seem.

Can two women find enough common ground for love or will their two different worlds and cultures keep them apart?

CPSIA information can be obtained
at www.ICGtesting.com
Printed in the USA
LVHW090932110720
660407LV00002B/387

9 781939 062055